MESSAGE TO BLACK MALE TEENZ IN AMERICA

Written by:

Paul J. Austin

MESSAGE TO BLACKMALE
TEENZ IN
AMERICA

Written by
Paul J. Austin

Copyright © 2012 by Paul J. Austin

All rights reserved. No part of this book may be reproduced or transmitted in any form or by any means, electronic, or mechanical, including photocopying, recording, or by any information storage and retrieval system, without permission in writing from the author.

Author's contact information:
P.O. Box 3243
Columbus, Georgia 31903
paultyner@ymail.com

Cover Artwork: VersusCompany.com

Special Dedication

My beloved parents: Mr. Claude W. Austin, Jr., and Mrs. Louise T. Austin; maternal grandparents: Mr. Jessie Tyner, and Mrs. Josie M. Tyner; paternal grandparents: Mr. Claude W. Austin, Sr., and Mrs. Johonnie Mae Austin. I love them forever. I love very much, also, my great grandparents from both sides. And on and on!

My favorite comrade, Mr. James Tyner, also known as Uncle Bubba. I love him. My beloved children: sons Shawn Austin,; and Michael Austin; daughters Kenyetta Austin; and Nakeia Austin. My beloved grandchildren: Jawuanna Austin; Torionna Austin; Asia Austin; Darius Austin; Shawntel Austin; Kayla Austin; Nattalie Austin; William Austin; Kyia Austin; Zoey Austin; and Kingston Austin. I love them all equally and very much.

A special dedication to Ms. Linda Joyce Wiggins! I will say that Linda is very dear to me! And there will always be a special place in my heart for her! My queen, rest in peace! I miss you!

Contents

Special Dedication iii
Introduction 1
Chapter 1 This Day 13
Chapter 2 The Black Male Teen 18
Chapter 3 Destructive Matters 21
Chapter 4 Guns 24
Chapter 5 An Important Message 26
Chapter 6 Wicked Legislation 31
Chapter 7 Korupt Kourts 34
Chapter 8 Piss-Ant-Hill 36
Chapter 9 Please Pull Your Pants Up 38
Chapter 10 Mis-Education Part 1 41
Chapter 11 Mis-Education Part 2 44
Chapter 12 History of A People 47
Chapter 13 William Lynch 50
Chapter 14 Emancipation Proclamation 53
Chapter 15 Slavery 56
Chapter 16 Unity 60
Chapter 17 Save the Children 63
Chapter 18 Loving Everybody 66
Chapter 19 The Greatest Love of All 70
Chapter 20 Baby Land 73
Chapter 21 Destroy the Black Male Child by Any Means Necessary 75
Chapter 22 Trayvon Martin Part 1 78

Chapter 23 Trayvon Martin Part 2 81

Chapter 24 Florida 85

Chapter 25 Rap Music 88

Chapter 26 The Athlete 92

Chapter 27 Dead Man Walking, Part 1 95

Chapter 28 Dead Man Walking, Part 2 98

Chapter 29 The Picture of Life 100

Chapter 30 Constitutional Rights 103

Chapter 31 Nigger! Nigga! Nigger! Nigga! 108

Chapter 32 Organizations 112

Chapter 33 Korrupt-Klandestine-Konspiracy 115

Chapter 34 The Grand Jury 118

Chapter 35 The Jury 121

Chapter 36 Debt Never Paid 125

Chapter 37 Evil-minded Judges 127

Chapter 38 News Media 130

v

Introduction

The sole purpose of this book is to show the teen Blackmales that that destructive and murderous path that they are on only leads to two unavoidable places. One place is a hellhole-plantation-prison! The other one is the graveyard! The author prays that reminding them of the FINAL DESTINATION PLACE being a PRISON, or the GRAVEYARD, will somehow help to persuade them to change their course! And get on the path of constructive-matters.

Georgia's prisons are overflowing with teen Blackmales, and some will never get a second chance to return to society. So they will die in one of those hellhole-plantation-prisons. Georgia, to my knowledge, has the toughest laws and penalties. They have the death penalty! Then life without parole! Life with parole, but must first serve thirty years, before becoming eligible! Then life with parole, but must first serve thirty years, before becoming eligible! And please note, you will not make the first or second parole considerations! And each set-off is eight more years! Then the sentences of ten, twenty, thirty, forty, or fifty years! Must be served without the benefit of parole.

Paul J Austin

There are countless teen Blackmales in the County jails throughout Georgia, that are waiting to stand trial. While the other ones are waiting to be transferred into the prison system. And all Georgia is doing is building more and more prisons! And adding new buildings to the prisons that they already have. For the most part, Georgia is a prison State/Colony. And if you do a little research you will learn that it always has been a prison colony! The Prison-Industry-Complex, has become a BIG BUSINESS, in the United States. Just as CHATTEL SLAVERY was!

The birth-control laws from Chattel Slavery, are still in effect. You see, by warehousing in large-mass-numbers teen Blackmales in their plantation-prisons. They cannot make babies!!! So there can be absolutely no reproduction of the race! Moreover, if the teen Blackmales don't get off of their destructive paths of senseless murders and other gruesome crimes there will manifest a lost generation for the future.

This Korrupt-Konspiracy, to lock-up the teen Blackmales and throw away the key, doesn't rest only with two hundred years behind time, Georgia. That KONSPIRACY, extends throughout Amerika. And teen Blackmales, the senseless murders that you are committing yearly, upon other teen Blackmales, is without a doubt, helping the KONSPIRATORS, in their wicked and evil plan to erase the Black Race, from the planet altogether!!! A REALITY!!!

Being in a hellhole-plantation-prison is not like living at the Hotel California. Poor medical care, and if you get a serious injury from a stabbing or playing sports, nine times out of ten the horse doctor will let you die. You can't wear tennis shoes from eight A.M. until four P.M., Monday thru Thursday. Poorly cooked, artificial foods and served in small portions. Five dollars for each medical or dental visit. The Department of Corrections takes a dollar and seventy five cents from each money order you receive, a four dollar fee for each disciplinary report you receive, and the guards frequently write them.

The two man cells, prison officials recently added another bunk and locker. The cell was already too small for two inmates. So it's definitely too small for three inmates! The open dormitory once housed fifty inmates, additional beds and lockers were added, now there's eighty inmates. Over-crowdedness in every way! And it is a fire hazard because it violates the fire safety laws. But the Safety Fire Kommissioner, and the State Fire Marshal, have refused to do their job to force the prison Kommissioner, to down-size all of the over-crowded prisons.

The segregation, lock-down, units which are supposed to have one person per cell! Prison officials are forcing two inmates per cell. To my knowledge, at least five inmates have murdered their cellmates. And there have been countless assaults, and rapes, due to prison officials' evil and wicked actions. Both the federal and state Kourts are aware of these evil practices. And they have refused to intervene and stop it. There is much, much more evil and wickedness.

Paul J Austin

I have a question, is prison where you teen Black Brothers chose to be??? Please note that this book is not solely for TEENS, but ADULTS, too!!! Which design is to bring together the parents and the child/children to read it together. And thereafter hold some discussions about the issues that the author embarks upon. The book is written in concise, short form, so the chapters are not very long, which makes it easier to read! I wrote it that way in the hopes that the reader will be inclined to read it more than once. And will be inclined to do some research on the things that I have stressed.

Notwithstanding the short chapters, a lot is being covered. I have also made reference to other books that will support some of what I am saying. I hope that the reader will enjoy this book because I come with a genuine intent. And I'm aware that some of the issues will undoubtedly bring out different emotions. But my primary mission is: The Teens Must Be Saved!!! And that is just a fundamental and colorable reality!

I concede that it is Universal Law, and therefore a duty for every race of people to diligently endeavor to save their race of children. And no one today is in more desperate need of being SAVED, than the Black teens of Amerika. Especially the teenage males. For they are murdering each other yearly, by the thousands! And some people believe it to be a curse, while others believe it to be the direct result of a Korrupt-Klandestine-Konspiracy!

It is not pseudoscience, but an undisputed concrete fact, that without the male, a race cannot reproduce itself. It is also a concrete fact, that Blacks make up only twelve percent of the

Amerikan population. While Blacks simultaneously make up approximately eighty percent of all plantation-prisons in Amerika. And that is both Federal and State institutions. Mis-education, dis-education, inferior-education, disenfranchisement, low self-esteem, self-hate, broken homes, lower development homes, jobless, homeless, and crime, among other things, play a major role in this road of destruction that the Black male teen find himself entangled in.

A lot of people have given up all hope and thrown in the towel. They stress that this is generation XXX, or the lost generation. Perhaps they are right that there is no hope? But on the contrary, perhaps they are wrong? Therefore, people must be willing to come back to the table and work to find a way to save generation XXX! And of course, all of them won't be saved, but it's better to save some, than to not save any.

First the people must confront those wicked, evil, and diabolical so-called legislators, or lawmakers, who are the biggest crooks in the world. Anyway, they must be forced to reverse and abolish those wicked laws that say: the parents cannot chastise their child/children. And the law that says grandparents don't have rights to their grandchildren. Then the people should go to the days of our Ancestors, when the parents, grandparents, other relatives, friends, and the community all raised the children! And in my mind, that will be instrumental in changing the murderous ways of the Black teenage males.

Paul J Austin

When I was growing up love was all over the community! Now today you find hate all over the community. Therefore, something is outrageously wrong. The Black community now is like a preternatural environment. Which in part is derived from the people not being user-friendly, and unified anymore. Neighbors, not speaking! And the children not playing together! The people have put themselves in prison in their own homes. When I was growing up, the neighbors not only spoke, they frequently visited each other. And the children always played together. And most of the time we were depleted when we got home. So we would eat, take a bath, and go to bed.

Children of today, most of the time, have to play in the house and with his/her brother(s) and sister(s), which I am sure gets boring. And if he/she doesn't have any siblings it has to be triple boring! The parents, or parent, say it's too dangerous for the child/children to go outside and play. Well that may be true in some cases, but for the most part, a lot of parents have allowed this bourgeoisie mentality to take over.

No one has the right to take away the children's rights to be children! Theirs is a Universal Human Right. Children have the right to play together and to exhaust themselves while playing together. In doing so, it is healthier for the children because, it will cut down on violence. Moreover, in most instances, the children will be so delighted to come together to play, that playing will be the only thing on their mind! The parents need desperately to come together and find a solution which will bring into existence a bilateral relationship for the people in the community to start back communicating! So that the children can start back playing together!

It is momentously important for the parents and other relatives to start teaching the children to read at an early age. It is irrefutable that reading expands the mind. For the most part, the children need to know the true history of our Ancestors, and the school's curriculum is not teaching them that. The school curriculum's primary focus is European history. Consequently, in a lot of cases, it makes Black children develop an inferiority complex, coupled with emotions of anger and hate for self. Because the school's curriculum paints a bogus and artificial picture that Black people made no contributions to civilization and humanity.

The children need to know that our Ancestors built great civilizations long before their kidnappers came into Mother Africa, and kidnapped them. And even to this day, other nations still model themselves after the civilizations that our Ancestors built. The children also need to know that our Ancestors, even while Slaves, contributed to building Amerika, and making it what it is today! Moreover, the school teachers are not gonna tell them that. Because as I have stressed, it's not part of the school's curriculum! On the contrary, if the children can study and get that additional teaching at home, I am sure that that will give them high self esteem, self worth, and make them proud of being Black! Inter alia.

The children must also be taught the value of life. They must come to know that life is very precious and that everyone has only one life to live. Even teenagers! They must come to know that it is wrong to kill! And that when one young Black Brother murders another young Black Brother, that he has done a very bad thing. And that nothing in the world can bring that dead brother back.

Those teenage Black Brothers must also be taught that the senseless murder of a teenage brother brings on a lot of hurt and pain for two families. The murdered brother's family is devastated, and profoundly hurt, because their son is gone and will never come home again! Then the brother that did the murder, his family is also devastated and profoundly hurt, because their son is sent to prison to serve a life sentence, in which he must serve thirty years, before becoming eligible for parole. And he surely won't make the first parole consideration! So he must serve eight more years! On the contrary, he may just get life without parole, and therefore never get out of prison!

Black male teenagers, you all must stop the madness of senselessly murdering each other. The authorities love what you all are doing; that way, one goes to the graveyard, and the other one goes to prison. Thousands are murdered yearly, and that certainly accommodates their Genocide-Plan!

It is sad that a Black child was murdered and his family can't get justice from this so-called justice-judicial-machine. Moreover, the senseless murder of Trayvon Martin, was racially motivated! His Black skin! I submit to you if Trayvon was Caucasian/White, he would still be alive. The fascist, murderer's action also constitutes malice afore thought! Because he stalked Trayvon, and even after being told by the police dispatcher to not get out of the car!!! He got out of the car anyway, and murdered Trayvon!!!

Now the right wing, ultra-conservative News Media is trying to paint a picture indicating Trayvon as the aggressor. They now are focusing on Trayvon's height and weight; ht. 5'11" and wt., 150 lbs. Consequently, it doesn't matter if he was the same ht., and size of Andre the Giant, a former wrestler who was 7'4" and 500 lbs. There was nothing that Trayvon could do up against a car and a gun that shoots nine times!!! Plus, Trayvon only had a cup of tea, and a bag of skittles in his hand! The racist, mainstream news media has gotten away from the main issues in the case, and that is that Trayvon was singled out and murdered exclusively due to his black skin! Which also makes it a HATE CRIME!!!

Another mockery of justice is the fascist, Klanpig judge releasing the vicious, callous, and malignant-hearted murderer, on a one hundred and fifty thousand dollar bond. He might as well have allowed him to sign a signature bond. I know several guys in Columbus, Georgia whose bond was higher than that for shoplifting. That rate of a bond for the murderer, in my mind, is a crystal clear picture that a conviction for him is as far away as the sun is from the earth! Ninety-three million miles!!!

Coupled with the aforementioned, hundreds and perhaps thousands of people are donating money to the racist, heartless and faceless murderer, to accommodate him with his defense. In other words, they are extending praise to him, and saluting him for murdering an unarmed Black child!!! I truly sympathize with Trayvon's family. I can just imagine the deep-seated hurt that they are experiencing. I have said the beforehand before, and I will simply say it again, "WE ARE ALL TROY DAVIS!!!"

And speaking of Mr. Troy Davis, whom was murdered by Georgia's Governor, whom signed the death warrant for the murder to be carried out, the United States Supreme Kourt, and the Georgia Supreme Kourt, whom refused to stop the murder. And there are others involved. My point here is to show you the evil, wickedness, and mercilessness of those people!!!

Seven of the nine witnesses against Troy re-canted their statement and testimony. And that was more than enough of a reason to release Troy, or to at least have given him a new trial. Consequently, the Pope is one of the most recognized religious figures in the World, and he asked them to not murder Troy, which availed naught! Then former Georgia's Governor, and President of the United States, Mr. Jimmy Carter, pleaded with them to not murder Troy, all to no avail. Notwithstanding the aforementioned innumerable other people's pleas to not murder Troy, were all ignored.

On the contrary, the system refuses to bring the confessed murder of Trayvon Martin, to justice! But they acted with jet speed to arrest, convict, and send Michael Vick to prison for killing a dog that he never killed! And dog fighting did not start with Michael Vick, and it damn sure won't end with Mr. Vick. The aforementioned is crystal clear, that a dog has more rights in Amerika, than a Black child!!

A lot of people here in Georgia express disgust and disappointment because they say that the present President of the United States, Mr. Barack Obama, didn't say anything, nor do anything, to prevent Mr. Troy Davis from being murdered. Well, I understand their position and I have to agree with them. Especially from what I hear and that is: that the elected officials in Georgia don't acknowledge Mr. Obama as the President, and neither do the majority of the citizens.

Black People, I have said this before and I will simply reiterate, please encourage your child/children to read! Reading is good for the soul. Reading expands the mind, and causes you to learn things you didn't know. Things that are imperative, and important that you know!

Let me clarify an important matter. I am not a RACIST! I am only a REALIST! Accordingly, I am wholly aware that all Caucasian/White people did not approve, and did not participate in the slave-trade. I am also aware that a lot of Caucasian/Whites were murdered by slave masters and their posses for helping slaves escape. As a matter of fact, Mr. John Brown, abolitionist, born 1800 and was murdered in 1859. He was a Caucasian, and he was opposed to the slave-trade. And he is one of Amerika's most renowned abolitionists. He aided Slaves escape, and that's why he was murdered. They claimed that he seized Harpers' Ferry in 1959.

Ms. Ida is Caucasian/White, and she is founder of the organization known as Caucasians United for Reparations and Emancipation for Black People. The organization is here in Amerika, and they are trying to get the United States Government to acknowledge their wrong in the slave-trade!!! And to pay the just due of REPARATIONS to the offspring of former Slaves!!! Moreover, Ms. Ida and her organization, to my knowledge, have been part of the ongoing struggle with Black People here in Amerika for more than twenty years. I often wonder will the U.S. Government ever concede the unjustified tragedy of CHATTEL SLAVERY!!!

I pray that this book will serve as an eye opener, and a guide-post to encourage young Black people to Read!!! AND TO READ MORE!!! May God be with all of us!!!

Chapter 1
This Day

    This is a sad day; this is a dreadful day; this is a hurtful day; this is a day like no other day before; this is a day that I never wanted to see; this is a day that I never would've fathomed in a million years. This is a day where too many to be counted young Black males hate their Black father! This is a day where too many to be counted young Black males hate themselves! This is a day where too many to be counted young Black males only see each other as the enemy! This is a day where too many to be counted young Black males are extremely un-educated and mis-educated! This is a day where too many to be counted young Black males find it convenient to murder each other! This is a day where a KORRUPT, KLANDESTINE, KONSPIRACY, is in place to bring the Black Race to GENOCIDE! This is a day where too many to be counted young Black males are locked away in a plantation-prison!

    This is a day that remonstrates that our Ancestors who fought and died for freedom, justice, equality, political, social, and economic emancipation for their futures, and the futures of generation, did it all for nothing! This is a day that our Ancestors have got to be crying out from their graves for the young Black Brothers, to stop murdering each other! This is a day that even Mother Earth is crying out for the young Black Brothers to stop murdering each other! This is a day like no other time in the history of Amerika! This is a day where the Black People's in Amerika's future is an uncertainty! This is a day where young Black Males are being buried yearly by the thousands! This is a day that should have never come to pass! This is a day where races of other people have put their guns on the shelf and are sitting back enjoying the show of seeing young Black Brothers murder each other for trivial, and avoidable matters!

  This is a day that must be reversed! This is a day where the elderly Blacks in the community are not talking to the young Black males out of fear of being beaten and murdered! This is a painful day! This is a cold, cold day! This is a day that I can't wear the color red or blue because if I do, I will be murdered! This is a bloody day! This is a day where death is with the young Black males, with every step that they take! This is a day that there appears to be no hope for the Black youths! This is a day that it doesn't have to be this way! This is a day where young Black males take for granted the value of life! This is a day where young Black males haven't realized that everybody has only one life to live! This is a day where young Black males don't want to enjoy longevity of life! This is a day where young Black males choose death over life! This is a day where there appears to be no opportunity for change in sight! This is a day where young Black males are profoundly in love with death!

This is a day of blackout! This is a day of misadventure! This is a day of frustration! This is a day of no peace! This is a day where school class rooms are vacant! This is a day of the walking mentally dead Black teenage Brothers! This is a day where the young Black Brothers refuse to listen to the voices of reason! This is a day where wrong is made to be right! This is a day where bullets are flying from all angles in the Black community! This is a day where death can't get no rest! This is a day where the death of young Black males is the order of the day! This is a day of no wedding bells! This is a day of unhappiness! This is a day of no tomorrow! This is a day when a lot of Black People wish that they were never born! This is a day wherein young Black Women can't get pregnant because their mate is dead, or in prison! This is a day of no procreation! This is a day that the graveyards are saying please don't bring anymore young Black Brothers in here! This is a day of in harm's way! This is a death day!

This is an unpleasant day! This is a non-loving day! This is a day of nightmare! This is a frightful day! This is a day that Mother Earth wants to throw up the countless bodies of the Black young males that are overflowing in her, but Mother Earth can't because they are dead! This is a day that wasn't foreseen! This is a day that just won't go away! This is a day that the birds are crying!

This is a day where young Black males are overflowing the graveyards as opposed to the colleges! This is a day where the young Black Brothers have become faceless, heartless, and bloodthirsty! This is a day of senseless killings! This is a day where young Black Brothers haven't realized that humans only have one chance at life! This is a day where young Black Brothers haven't realized that once a person is pronounced dead, nothing can be done to bring him back! This is a day where young Black Brothers haven't realized that they had better hold on to life as long as they can! This is a day where precious life ends before it begins! This is a day that has the Angels terrified! This is a day that even Jesus didn't foresee! This damn day! This is a day that isn't the way it's supposed to be! This is a very dark day! This is a day of a living hell! This is a day that none of our Ancestors prayed to see! This is a day that must go away! This is a day that brings about sorrow and pity! This is a day that brings about crying and mourning! This is a day that shatters all hopes and dreams! This is a day where another young Black Brother was just buried and he was gunned down for no reason by another young Black Brother! This is a day where all of the Black Mothers are crying because their teenage son is dead! This is a day where you young Black Brothers need to change your way of thinking!

    Please listen carefully Black teenage Brothers! This is a day where if you all don't stop murdering each other, you are going to find yourselves EXTINCT! In other words, removed from the planet altogether! You now have this chance to wake-up, before it is too late!!! This is the day!!!

Chapter 2
The Black Male Teen

The beforehand is derived from observation and experience. The Black male child of today is suffering from depression due to an extreme identity crisis, which has created a disease inside of him, and its primary source is that he is being forced to grow up without his father! I grew up with my father in my life until he was murdered, when I was in my early teens. Daddy was a loving and great person, and he had knowledge and wisdom. And mere words are not sufficient for me to express how much I love and miss daddy!

A father is more than just a man! He is someone whom vouchsafe, and takes care of his family. He has knowledge and wisdom. So he is not just strong physically, but most importantly, he is strong mentally! He believes in family Unity, and does what it takes to assure that the family is unified! Most fathers, to include mine, won't whip their child/children, when the child does something inappropriate. Moreover, he will sit the child down and talk to him. And that is also because a father is wise, and he understands that a child has a universal human right to be a child. So the trivial things that children often do is expected of them. And for the most part, the father loves his child/children very much! And he demonstrates it!

Today's society is different, and a large number of young Black males deeply hate and despise their Black father, for one reason or another. Consequently, this has taken on a domino effect, which has caused him to hate himself; while in the process of hating his father! And it doesn't just stop there. He now hates every other Black man or child.

The aforementioned is just part of the reason why young Black males act without due deliberation, to rush and murder each other. They only see each other as the enemy! So when he murders his Black Brother, to him he has only killed a fly! Thereafter, a lot of them will laugh and brag on how he murdered his young brother. And he murdered him because of his Black skin!!

Young Black Brothers, please stop the madness of murdering another young Black teenager. You are only hurting yourself, and your race! One of you goes to an unwarranted early grave, the other one goes to a hellhole prison environment! And as he gets older, he will regret it. Because he will spend the rest of his life there! Or at least the best years of his life there! That is only if he is not murdered by the guards or other prisoners.

Paul J Austin

I submit to you young Brothers, that it is time for a CHANGE! So I am asking you to start with the Black Male teen in the mirror!!! MAKE A CHANGE TODAY!!!

Chapter 3
Destructive Matters

It is an irrefutable fact, that too many to be counted young Black Males are caught up in destructive matters. Crime, drugs, and alcohol which leads to their final destination of only two places: "Prison or the Graveyard!" Young Brothers, life is not to be taken for granted, and you only have one chance at life! Life can also be a wonderful thing. But you all are gonna have to make the decision to stop participating in those things that are inevitably going to take life away from you at a precious young age! Prison and the graveyard!

Consequently, it doesn't have to be that way for you young Brothers. Because you all have a choice. And you can choose constructive matters. Read books that will open up your mind and make you worldly-wise! Stay in school, and once completed go to college. And you will be way ahead of some of the other students if you read the right books! You'll be able to separate the truth from the falsehood. And that will certainly make a significant difference in your educational growth and development.

Teenage Black Brothers, in order to accomplish the aforementioned, you all must stop the madness of murdering each other! I want you to think about the following: "What other race of young people in Amerika are murdering each other like you all?" I will answer that question with certainty. Absolutely no other race of teenagers is murdering each other!!! Moreover, I can truly testify that when I was growing up, the Black teenage males were not murdering each other.

I must profess that this murderous-frenzy that you all have going on is novel and new, among other things. And for the most part it is untenable and wholly unjustified! I reiterate, there is nothing that you all can say that will justify one teenage brother murdering another teenage brother. And it has to stop! It must stop!

I concede that you all don't have to murder each other. As it is not part of the rules, for you all to live on this planet. And murder shouldn't even be part of your train of thought. I have another question. What is it that your brother does that makes you so angry that you have to murder him? Growing up! There were times when some of my friends, to include myself, that we fought with each other. And the best fighter won. Thereafter, we would shake hands and move on, or finish playing like nothing had happened.

And during those days, in which a lot of people refer to them as the good ole days. Anyway, we never even contemplated the issue of murdering each other. We also considered ourselves friends of family. Teen Black Brothers please avoid destructive-matters! And get on the road to constructive-matters! Please be aware that what you all are doing has the masses of the Amerikan people hating you. And you probably don't care, but you should care. Because it is not just a bad reflection on you teens! It is a bad reflection on all Black People! And you better be aware and careful, because a lot of other races of people here in Amerika are inclined to kill you wherever they see you! Right there on the spot! Because they see, and are well aware of what you all are doing to each other. So out of that fear, they're inclined to get you, before you get them!!!

I repeat, please stay away from DESTRUCTIVE-MATTERS, that is if you don't want to rest in an early grave. Or serve the rest of your life in an abyss-of-hell, plantation-prison!!! I must also repeat, that CONSTRUCTIVE-MATTERS are the right way to go. It is the only way to your salvation. And it is your LIFE-SAVER!!!

Chapter 4

Guns

Guns shatter hope! Guns halt prosperity! Guns terminate dreams! Guns ruin the lives of the shooter, and the one that is shot! I pray for the day to come when teenage brothers will put their guns down, and resolve their conflicts, if there are conflicts. Anyway, resolve it by walking away, or by cordial conversation. Moreover, that would be the wise and right thing to do. Because guns don't give to life, guns take away life!

Brothers of teenage years the time has arrived for you all to put down your guns, and pick up a book that will expand your mind so that you can see what is really going on! The day has arrived for you all to take your finger off of the trigger of a gun, and put your fingers on a computer. So that you can gather some knowledge from in and around this world that we live in.

We are living in the information age, and without knowledge of important matters that will awaken you from your mentally dead state, you will, without a doubt, find yourselves erased from the Planet Earth. Because without the right kind of knowledge, you will be lost and forgotten!!! Wake up now!!!

    I must profess, that murdering each other is not the answer to whatever it is that compels you all to murder each other. Moreover, Wisdom, Knowledge, and Understanding are the keys that will put an end to this murderous path that you all have so boldly taken. So put your hands on a book, as opposed to some bullets. And put your fingers on the keys of a computer, as opposed to the trigger of a gun!!!

Paul J Austin

Chapter 5

An Important Message

All prisons are a society within a society! Although things are a lot more difficult and complicated in a prison society. You are restricted on what you can eat. The prison commissary, for the most part, sells foods that are unwholesome. Things like saltine crackers, potato chips, corn chips, pork skins, honey buns, ramen noodle soups, cookies, cakes, and candy. Moreover, those aforementioned items are saturated with sodium, salt, and refined white sugar. And they will hasten one to an early grave!

Then the food in the chow hall is a monstrous joke! I mean it is ridiculous, and preposterous, the food that's being fed daily to the Georgia prisoners. Here's a synopsis: Most breakfast consists of grits or white cold potatoes, corn bread-sweet-muffins, and an orange or applesauce. Monday-Wednesday for lunch is a peanut butter and jelly sandwich, on white bread, and they even serve white bread to the diabetic prisoners! And it is a fact that white bread is detrimental towards good health! Wheat bread is the better bread. Also, man cannot live by bread alone! At least five times a week, the dinner meal consists of cornbread, collards, or turnip greens with pinto beans. Then, two days will be pinto beans and white rice or white potatoes. The whole menu lacks wholesome foods! Also all of the meats are filled with artificial ingredients! I'm a vegetarian.

Another reprehensible thing about Georgia, is those wicked and evil minded prison officials, and legislators don't allow the prisoners to be paid. So if one doesn't have loved ones or friends sending him money, that person has no choice but to eat that slave-like, garbage food. And I reiterate, the foods in the prison store are unwholesome!

One of the most diabolical, and unjustifiable, rules of law that those tyrannical dictators have is: when a loved one perishes, the prisoner is not allowed to attend the funeral, nor view the body. In my mind, it should be mandatory that a prisoner be allowed to pay his/her last respects to a loved one. That rule of law is wholly and completely unjustified! But it's part of the legislators, and prison official, neoslavery rules. I had been locked up twenty plus years when my beloved Mother perished in 2006, and of course, I was denied the Universal Human Right to attend her funeral.

Prison officials tell you when to go to bed and when to wake-up. You are forced to work on a detail, but you are not paid one red penny! And here in Georgia, the visitation is a travesty. Only twelve people are allowed to be on your visiting list, and they must be immediate family only: father, mother, child/children, brother, sister, wife or girlfriend. You are allowed to kiss your wife or girlfriend once upon entering the visiting room and once upon leaving. You are told where to sit, and you can't move from that chair, unless going to the restroom. You cannot hold, nor show any love or affection to your child/children.

The televisions are turned on Monday thru Thursday at 4:00 p.m., until 11:30 p.m.. One is for movies, the other one is for sports. They're in the same area, and I can't begin to tell you of the noise level from the televisions and the inmates. But it is indeed a pandemonium!

Georgia's prison industry complex is operating for the most, from Chattel Slavery, William Lynch, and Jim Crow laws and rules. And one of the things that they enjoy doing the most is beating and murdering handcuffed, non-resisting neoslave-prisoners! And of course, they get away with it. Just as the Chattel Slaves had no rights, the neoslave-prisoners don't have any rights! Although today, sometimes getting the beating or murder of a neoslave-prisoner out in the public, one or two guards may have to resign! Just to go and get hired at another plantation-prison. But they are never sent to prison!!! Also assaulting and murdering neoslave-prisoners is the most efficient way to promotions!!!

That evil villain, J. Wayne Garner, former prison Kommissioner, while in office, frequently gathered together a team of ferocious guards that he called the riot squad. And in spite of the fact that there were no riots! They would arrive at each prison that they hit about 4:00 a.m., and they went in, and beat unmercifully non-resisting inmates. While simultaneously destroying their properties. Those heinous and hideous acts occurred in the latter part of the nineteen nineties.

Derived from the aforementioned, those evil wardens put together a rule to carry on in former Kommissioner Garner's work. So now, without warning, a team of fierce guards at about 5:00 a.m., comes in the dorm screaming and yelling, "Don't say one word! Take off all of your clothes, and walk to the right!" There several officers will instruct you to hold up your genitals, turn around, spread your buttocks, and squat and cough. You are then forced to stand nude for at least two and a half hours, and in front of female guards, while other guards ransack your locker. And you aren't allowed to use the restroom.

While at Georgia State Prison in Reidsville, Georgia, which was the most dangerous prison in Georgia at the time, during the early nineteen eighties, when it was maximum security and high max, I was in two major shakedowns!!! Now for the last fifteen years I have been at medium and minimum security prisons, and I've been in far more shakedowns!!!

You can't make babies in prison. You can't raise and take care of your family from prison. You can't enjoy the finer things in life from prison. You can't live a normal life in prison. And you can't make important life decisions from prison. You can however, watch your life deteriorate and decay while in prison.

There is much, much more that I can stress about Georgia's abyss of hell, prison societies! But this isn't the book for that. So please read my book entitled: Injustice-N-Georgia, and get the full story, ok. Moreover, teen Black males, you have got to start reading more! There is a Konspiracy in place with many pitfalls aiming at you, to fall into prison or the graveyard!!!

Please note, a prison hellhole environment isn't a place for adults. So it certainly isn't a place for children. Therefore, I must emphatically stress to the teen Black males, to please stop committing unprovoked crimes! In order to avoid spending your entire life; or most of the best years of your precious life, in one of Amerika's hellhole plantation-prisons!!! You must learn to walk away, to circumvent getting caught up in the TRAP!!!

Chapter 6
Wicked Legislation

During former President Mr. Bill Clinton's time in office a wicked piece of legislation was passed that took things back to the sixteenth century, especially for prisoners. The legislation is known as "The Prison Litigation Reform Act"! That legislation has numerous functional parts. One part is it speeds up the death penalty sentence to be carried out for the prisoners on death row.

Another part, it makes it more difficult for state prisoners to have their habeas corpus petitions granted in federal Kourts. It also discourages a lot of state prisoners here in Georgia from ever filing a state habeas corpus, because the Georgia Kourts are illegally charging a two hundred dollar fee to file the petition, and most don't have $200.00.

Let me clarify to make clear what's going on. The Prison Litigation Reform Act has a clause in it that a state prisoner must pay a three hundred fifty dollar fee to be able to bring a lawsuit in federal Kourt against state officials. That is horribly wrong and wicked because, Georgia prisoners do not get paid one red penny for their slave-labor-work. Plus, forcing any prisoner to pay for filing a lawsuit is a form of stealing, double tax money. Anyway, the bill doesn't say anything about filing fees for a petition for a writ of habeas corpus, nor a petition for a writ of mandamus!

And Georgia drafted legislation from the Federal legislation and the official code of Georgia Annotated 42-12-3, makes clear that the petition for a writ of habeas corpus is not part of the law where prisoners must pay a filing fee. It also cost two hundred twenty dollars to file a writ of mandamus. The Georgia Kourts are deeply engaged in theft by taking, theft by deception, and other criminal activities by charging those fees for the filing of mandamus, and habeas corpus petitions.

Derived from the wicked and evil actions of the Federal Government to approve the Prison Litigation Reform Act legislation, the assaults and robbery of prisoners by prison guards has increased because, most prisoners don't have three hundred fifty dollars to file a lawsuit in state or federal Kourt. So filing lawsuits has decreased significantly. Moreover, while I was confined at Wilcox State Prison, in 2012, I was assaulted by two officers on the cert team, and robbed of twenty dollars in food items, and of forty two CD's, which totaled more than four hundred dollars.

There is another major problem that Georgia prisoners are faced with. That is the state and federal judges, at least the majority of them are working together in a Konspiracy with the prison officials. Moreover, the few prisoners that can afford to file a lawsuit for the most part, are disinclined to do so because, they are aware that they can't win! Because the legislators, prison Kommissioners, prison wardens, the Kourts, and the Governor, and those behind the scenes have all given the guards the approval to rob and assault the prisoners.

Chapter 7
Korupt Kourts

Teen Brother, when you pull that trigger on that gun and murder someone, I want you to fully understand that the Kourt system is not gonna be lenient with you. So just be prepared to spend the rest of your life in hell, plantation-prison! Or the best years of your life behind the bars. Like all of your twenties, thirties, and forties! And it could go beyond your forties.

Ninety nine percent of all direct appeals are denied. Especially here in Way-Down-in-Dixie Land, Behind-the-Times, Georgia. So your chances of being granted a new trial, are zero percent. And it can take from six to eight years just to exhaust the direct appeal process. And all you can do is hold on to a ray-of-hope, while waiting for that Kourt decision, that nine times out of ten will say, DENIED!

You can then file a petition for a writ of habeas corpus, seeking to have your conviction overturned and be awarded a new trial. Moreover, ninety-nine percent of all petitions for a writ of habeas corpus are denied. And I repeat, especially here in two hundred years Behind-the Times, Georgia. Moreover, you must file the petition for a writ of habeas corpus immediately after the final level on direct appeal is denied. Because if you let a year pass before you file the writ of habeas corpus, you will be time barred, which means, if you are denied relief in the State Kourts, you won't be allowed to file a petition for a writ of habeas corpus in the Federal Kourts.

I am a living testimony that the Kourt system is Super-Korrupt, Racist, Wicked, and Evil. I have been confined in a Georgia hellhole-plantation-prison for the last thirty years! And they have, with malice, denied me justice in both State, and Federal, Kourts! In spite of the overwhelming concrete evidence that shows that I am INNOCENT!!! For more information, and proof, please read my book: INJUSTICE-N-GEORGIA!!!

You must also remember that, "We are all Troy Davis!" And the only difference between Mr. Troy Davis and others, like myself, is: Those Wicked, evil minded, black-hearted villains murdered Troy under what they call a death sentence. Moreover, they want to murder the rest of us the same way. But the Government hasn't given them the approval yet!!! So in the meantime, we are allowed to languish in hell-prisons, until we die!!!

Chapter 8

Piss-Ant-Hill

Teenage Black Brothers, you come to prison in your teens and early twenties, but you don't leave at the same age that you come in. No, you will be in your late forties, late fifties, or late sixties, and there are plenty of times when people don't leave these abyss-of-hell, plantation-prisons alive!

I want you to read carefully what I am about to write, and I want you to thoroughly think about it for several minutes. Then ask yourself, is that really what you desire? I know numerous prisoners that died before being released, and most of them had served more than twenty years. A few had even served more than thirty years. Consequently, their family, the ones that were left, and for most of them their parents had died, so a brother, sister, uncle, aunt, or cousin were their only surviving relatives, refused, for whatever reason, to accept their body for burial. I've been told that a funeral today cost ten thousand dollars or more. Maybe they didn't have the money for burial?

Moreover, whenever that happens, the State will bury the prisoner. The burial site is in Reidsville, Georgia, and the prison cemetery is known as PISS-ANT-HILL! And I submit to you that no one should have to be buried in that cemetery. Prison officials have you put in a pine box, and you are then put in that burial ground. A white cross is then stood up over your grave. Teen Black Brothers, there are white crosses as far as the eyes can see. The crosses have no name upon them, so no one can visit your grave site to sweep it off, or put a flower on it.

My main point is, if you don't have family members alive that will maintain a decent burial insurance policy for you, if you die in prison, you will be buried in PISS-ANT-HILL. Accordingly, there are prison cemeteries in every state throughout the United States of Amerika. So the same applies to every teenager, in whatever state you dwell in. I say to all of the teenagers that it is not too late! Please, right now, stop the madness! Please, right now, stop the senseless killings!!! Moreover, the life you save, will be your own!

Chapter 9
Please Pull Your Pants Up

Young Black Brothers, I am making a vociferated outcry to you all too please pull your pants up! Stop acting like savages, and uncivilized brute beasts, ok. you make people of other races hate you even more by walking around with your pants hanging off of your buttocks. You profess that you are a man, but men don't walk around in the public with their pants hanging off of their buttocks.

There is no legitimate reason that you can give for walking around with your pants hanging off of your buttocks. The people in authority have made laws to fine you, and to put you in prison for walking around with your pants hanging off of your buttocks.

Walking around with your pants hanging off of your buttocks shows that you don't know who you are! You remind me of the lion in the movie The Lion King. He didn't know he was a King, so hanging out with a pig made him believe that he was a pig! Therefore, he started eating and acting like a pig. Moreover, you certainly can't assume the position as a King with your pants hanging off of your buttocks!

Walking around with your pants hanging off of your buttocks shows that you don't have any self respect, nor respect for others in your midst! To include your parents and grandparents, because I'm sure that they don't walk around with their pants hanging off of their buttocks.

There are those that stress that they walk around with their pants hanging off of their buttocks to make a statement. Well, what statement are you making? Is it one of asinine analphabetic, and functioning below the threshold of conscious awareness and perception? Even an infant doesn't want his pamper hanging off of his buttock, and that is why you don't see it hanging off of him.

Youthful Black males, what is going through your mind that makes you think that it is ok to walk around with your pants hanging off of your buttocks? Why do you think that people want to see your foul-smelling, rear-end nakedness??? To sum it up in a nutshell, people don't appreciate you exposing your foul-smelling, rear-end nakedness, and people certainly don't want to see your foul-smelling, rear-end nakedness!

Youthful Black Brothers, will you pledge allegiance, that from this day forward you will pull your pants up? Remember, you are not that pig! You are a King! Therefore, let the world know that you are civilized, and worthy of living among the other civilized people of the earth!

I repeat, youthful Black Brothers, please pull up your pants! FOR GOD'S SAKE, PLEASE PULL UP YOUR PANTS!!! IT IS NOT HARD TO DO!!!

Chapter 10

Mis-Education Part 1

I have underwent Conscious-Raising and through that method, I've been raised to a living perpendicular! So for the most part, I am self-educated. I'm aware that our Ancestors were kidnapped from many parts of what is today known as Africa. Accordingly, our Ancestors were brought here to be slaves, and in being made slaves, they were stripped of their family names, and given a name like Doug Smith, Tom Johnson, Johnny Tyler, or Mike Williams, just to name a few. Those last names still, today, tie us to Slavery! The education system, inter alia, has made most of us ashamed to be acknowledged as Black, and there are some who wouldn't dare take on the name of their Ancestors!

In being made slaves, our Ancestors were stripped of their heritage, culture, and ways of life. They were forced through murders and other horrific human rights violations to submit to their captor's ways of eating and lifestyles, which were not conducive to their well-being. Another egregious thing that the

Slavemasters did, is they stripped our Ancestors of their Native tongue, and one great man call that method Civil Death! You see, by stripping us of our Native tongue, it caused us to lose our Universal Correct way to communicate, and understand, each other!

    This education system has maliciously failed the Blacks. Especially the young Black Males. The system teaches European History ways of life and values. It misleads Black children into believing that our Ancestors made no contributions to humanity. That presentation is as far away from the truth, as the sun is from the earth. Ninety-three million miles! That monumental lie has also caused some black children to develop an inferiority complex and low self-esteem.

    The above method has also caused a lot of young Black males to become uninterested, discontent, and irate. Consequently, followed by the inevitable: Drop out. As a matter of fact, the dropout rate for Black males is at an all time high, and there are more young Black males today, that are trapped inside of those hellhole-prison-plantations, throughout Amerika, than are in college! The aforementioned is all derived from the quintessence of a Wicked, Korrupt, Klandestine Konspiracy, which must be reversed! Unless the Black race wants to be caught up in Genocide?!

    Black people need to educate themselves in extracurricular matters if they are not already educated that way. Then, they need to start educating their child/children at home. That way the children will recognize the misinformation that is being taught to them at school. On the contrary, parents need to also rally and protest until the school system gets an equal amount of text books on Blacks, to show our achievements and intellectual advancements. Our Ancestors built great civilizations before their ghastly, nemesis, and abhorrent kidnapping! Also, some of our Ancestors were Kings and Queens.

    Educators also need to add the textbook, which is entitled The Official Code of Georgia Annotated: Title 16, here in Behindhand Georgia. It is the book that sets out the crimes, and penalties, therefore in the state, and that is only the right thing to do. Moreover, children will then know what acts will constitute a crime, and they will know the penalty (sentence length) if convicted of the crime! In my mind, that method of education will deter a lot of senseless murders and other crimes. But the way it is today, a child not knowing what constitutes a crime, is a blatant and atrocious act of entrapment by your elected officials!

Chapter 11
Mis-Education Part 2

In this chapter I will give a synopsis on some of the crimes and penalties therefore. And please try to understand that the beforehand are some of the things that the children need to know. Hopefully, through the grace of God, it will deter and stop them altogether from committing unprovoked and senseless crimes of outrage and abominable proportion.

It is my platonic-reality that being Black in Amerika, that you are guilty of a crime even while still in the womb of the mother. Here in Georgia, one murder can take place, and you and five teenagers are arrested, in spite of the evidence showing that there was one gun, and one triggerman! All five of them will be charged with malice murder. Moreover, conviction is unavoidable, even when there is no evidence to convict. You must know that the jury is the neolynch mob! The death sentence, life without parole, or life with parole are the penalties for malice murder. Even if you receive life with parole, you must serve thirty years before you become eligible for parole, and you probably won't make the first parole! Then an eight year set-off follows the denial!

Here in Antediluvian Times, Georgia, your wife or girlfriend can engage in consensual sex with you and two days later, if she gets angry with you and say that you raped her, you will be arrested, tried, and convicted, and sentenced to life without parole, or life with parole. Remember, life with parole is thirty years to serve before eligibility for parole. Even if she comes back to the Kourt a year later and says that she was angry and lied, it won't help. You will still have to serve the time.

On the contrary, a strange woman can say that a man wearing a mask raped her, and that she may be able to identify him by voice. If you are arrested, you will be convicted! This can happen even if there is no DNA evidence, and no other concrete evidence.

Here in Behindhand Georgia, the crime of kidnapping carries the penalty of life without parole, or life with parole. The law states that: a person commits the crime of kidnapping when they abduct, and steal way, the person! I submit to you that there are too many prisoners to be counted that were convicted of kidnapping. The D.A. is securing indictments for kidnapping, when a person goes into a store to rob, and he tells the clerk to move over one or two feet from the register!

Here in Georgia, you can be seventeen years old (still a child), and a fourteen or fifteen year old girl can say that she saw you urinating behind an abandoned house, and you will be arrested and convicted for child molestation. At the age of 17 years old, you can have consensual sex with a girl of 14 or 15 years old, and even if she is not a virgin, if she tells on you, you will be arrested and convicted for statutory rape. The penalty for those crimes is ten to twenty years, and to serve without parole.

There is about one hundred or more crime that young Black males can be sent to prison for, for a long time, and sometimes forever! Georgia has one hundred and fifty-nine counties, so the rise in the number of teen Black males that are being poured into those plantation-prisons is untenable, and unjustified. When you are unbeknownst of dangerous pitfalls, becoming a victim of it is unavoidable!

I also hope that you will agree with me that adding the book that set out the crimes and penalties as a textbook in every school system is a necessity. You see, in order to take a big step towards Saving the Children, the children must be made aware of the detrimental things they can get themselves into, and may never be able to get out of. The children must know that killing a human being is not the same as killing a fly or gnat.

Chapter 12
History of A People

The History of a people is of the highest degree of importance for them to know, because if you don't know your past, you certainly won't know your future! Moreover, this educational system has went to extreme measures to blindfold and chicane the Black youths, both male and female, from knowing about their past! That is part of the reason why the Black youths are in a state of topsy-turvy, and suffering from the state of an identity crisis.

The Black youths are unaware of the atrocities that were imputed upon their Ancestors during their captivity and sojourn to Slavery! During the trip of the Trans-Atlantic-Slave-Disaster, sometimes the ships were filled beyond capacity, so innumerable slaves were then thrown overboard to the sharks! Can you imagine for a minute, drowning, and being eaten, at the same time by merciless, carnivorous sharks? What a horrible and gruesome way to die!

This chapter will not cover the full spectrum of the atrocities that our Ancestors encountered during Horrendous-Chattel-Slavery! Consequently, that is supposed to be part of the school's Curriculum, to educate the Black youths about what occurred during slavery, and also about the greatness of our Ancestors. To include the great civilizations that they built long before their slavery misadventure, and about the contributions that the Slaves made in building Amerika, inter alia.

The Japanese children are taught in school that the Amerikan Government, on August 6, 1945, dropped the atomic bomb on Hiroshima, Japan, and on August 9 1945, dropped an atomic bomb on Nagasaki, Japan. Every other race of people whom suffered an atrocity by a foreign Government is taught in school about that particular history, along with all other important matters! Here in Amerika though, Black people have been tricked for decades about their history, and they are still, even in the present, being tricked! Also, due to the aforementioned, a lot of Black children have developed an inferiority complex for not knowing the greatness and worth of their Ancestors, and themselves.

I repeat that Black children, just like all other nationalities of children, have the right to know their history, and this deprivation of not being taught that particular history must be nipped in the bud! For starters, life did not start with Black people in Africa. Moreover, our Ancestors were settled in various parts of the earth long before that particular tribe went into what is called

Africa today. The Black man, and the Black woman, is the original inhabitants of the earth. Just do a little research.

Derived from the aforementioned, you should have learned that it takes more than one month to learn of the History of our Ancestors! Moreover, our History goes back millions of years! Reading is of paramount importance, because reading expands the mind! Some of the things you learn through reading not only amaze the mind, but it can also shock the mind, and it is so true that the mind is indeed, a terrible thing to waste! But there's a Korrupt-Klandestine-Konspiracy in place to assure that the Black youths are deprived of an adequate education.

Please be aware that this Korrupt-Klandestine-Konspiracy to deprive the Blacks of a thorough and accurate knowledge of our Ancestors, and the greatness of ourselves, did not start with this generation. Rather, it has been in place for four hundred fifty-some years!!! That was when our (Blacks) sojourn to Chattel Slavery started, in 1555!!!

The time is overdue! The time is now! Therefore, it is time for the Black People to demand that the Educators immediately stop teaching the Black Youths mis-education, dis-education, and an inferior-education, and teach them the True History of our Ancestors, as well as the true greatness of themselves!!!

HENCEFORTH, TRUE EDUCATION, AND TRUE HISTORY, and absolutely nothing short of that!

Chapter 13
William Lynch

I must state that I am extremely shocked to learn that there are too many to be counted Black male teens that have never read, and are not even aware of the book entitled: William Lynch, by William Lynch! William Lynch was a Slave-Master, and Slave-Owner from the West Indies, and he visited with his Slave-Master and Slave-Owner friends. His plan-program was, for the most part, designed to control the Slaves, and to turn the Slave against each other.

Slave-Master Lynch stated to his Slave-Master friends that if they would fully implement his program, that it would last for hundreds of years, or maybe even thousands of years. Because, he said, that once the Slave were indoctrinated, that they would pass their indoctrination down to the next generation, and that generation would do the same thing, and on, and on, and on!!!

Slave-Master Lynch's program has many parts, and I encourage you Black male teen Brothers to read the book.

Moreover, I will briefly go over a couple of parts from the book. Fear was one of his control measures, so he would take a slave-man and tie him between two horses, then hit both horses at the same time! With the horses running in different directions, they pulled the man in half, and the women and children were forced to watch that evil act!

Another method of Slave-Master Lynch's program was the tuning of the dark skinned Slave against the light skinned slave, and the light skinned slave against the dark skinned slave, the slave woman against the slave man, and the man slave against the woman slave. To this day you can see those wicked methods are part of the reason that there is so much hate among the Blacks here in Amerika.

Another part of Slave-Master Lynch's was/is to train the trust for each other out of them. Surely you can still see that today, because most Blacks in Amerika certainly do not trust each other. That is part of the reason for the disunity which is so overflowing. I repeat, please read the book: William Lynch, By William Lynch.

Black male Teens, I want you all to stop the madness and evilness of MURDERING EACH OTHER, AND CALLING EACH OTHER NIGGA, OR NIGGER all day and all night. That will show to the whole World that the William Lynch program is no longer with you.

Paul J Austin

I submit to you all that you must do it, and you must do it now! Otherwise, there will be no FUTURE for the BLACK RACE here in Amerika.

Chapter 14
Emancipation Proclamation

The signing of the Emancipation Proclamation that became effective January 1, 1863, did not free the Slaves! Moreover, signing a piece of paper without having something else of value to go along with it, was/is bootless. It would be like going to the bank to borrow some money, and your application is approved, but thereafter they don't give you any money, nor write you a check. I hope that you understand my point.

Notwithstanding the aforementioned, I am sure that a lot of people will be in discord with me, and they will argue that the signing of the Emancipation Proclamation did free the Slaves. Well, I will stand on top of Mount Everest, which is twenty nine thousand one hundred forty one feet high, and I will say that it didn't. Because, I know for a fact, that the signing of that piece of paper did not free the Slaves!

I will encourage you to do some research, but I will show some tangible evidence to support my position. Consequently, in order for a people to be free, they need some land! The culprits promised the Chattel Slaves forty acres and two mules, which they never received. Land is necessary, and a requisite to real freedom. Foremost, the people can establish a Government for their people, and by their people, and in doing that, they will be recognized like other Governments of the World.

    The kidnappers stripped our Ancestors of their true names. You see, whatever Slave-Master bought a Slave or Slaves, they became the property of that Slave-Master. So if his name was John Smith, all or the Slaves were given a name, with the last name being Smith. It is those last names that still tie Black People today, in Amerika, to SLAVERY!!!

    The kidnappers also stripped our Ancestors of their Mother tongue, and one remarkable and outstanding Brother calls that CIVIL DEATH. He stressed that when the captors stripped our Ancestors of their true language, that evil act was/is Civil Death, and he is correct! It basically murdered us as a people! It took away our human rights to be recognized as human beings!!!

    Consequently, with some land, our Ancestors would have established institutions of learning so that we would have regained our Ancestors names, and Mother tongue. Amerika is a multi-cultural society. To name a few: Cubans, Mexicans, Puerto Ricans, Chinese, Pilipino, Japanese, Russians, Germans, and French. A lot of them speak fluent English, but they still have their Ancestor's language, and I am sure that when they communicate in their language, they understand each other much better.

Message to BlackMale Teenz -N- America

I again repeat that signing that piece of paper, the Emancipation Proclamation, did not free the Chattel Slaves, and the Neo-Slaves have yet to be set FREE!!! Remember, READ, because you can learn a lot, because reading takes you out of that box! You become disillusioned, disabused, and Worldly-Wise from reading!

Chapter 15
Slavery

We Blacks have to always remember that SLAVERY in Amerika was never abolished! It only underwent a transfiguration, and that is from Chattel Slavery, to Neo-Slavery, derived from Neo-Colonialism! I want you to think about the following: Our Ancestors were kidnapped from their native homeland, and brought more than ten thousand miles to a strange land.

Consequently, they were stripped of their names, language, identity, customs, traditions, ways of eating, and other ways of life. The kidnappers forced their names, language, and ways of eating among other things, upon them, which was for the most part, not conducive to our Ancestors well-being. They were also forced to work for Centuries, for free, for the kidnappers and their offspring, coupled with being denied educational opportunities. Then, one day after approximately four hundred years later, the kidnappers' offspring tell our Ancestors, "You are free to go."!!! Well, where were they going to go, penniless, broke, and lost???

The crafty, artful, and shrewd Slave-Masters were well aware that they never had any genuine intentions to free the Slaves! Moreover, if their intentions were sincere, then they would have paid REPARATIONS to our Ancestors, and not just in the form of money! They would have also aided them in finding a piece of uncharted land, then aided them with equipment and other materials to cultivate the land, so that our Ancestors would've had a safe, and stable, home-base for their offspring.

If you would do just a small amount of research in regards to where one nation or more wronged another nation, you would discover that the nation that wronged the other nation, paid that nation REPARATIONS! A prime example: both times that Amerika attacked Iraq. After the war, they sent people to aid the Iraqi people in re-building the infrastructure of Iraq, and they also aided the Iraqi Government and their people in various other ways. Notwithstanding the aforementioned, the European settlers that took this country, called Amerika today, through bloodshed from the Indians. This Government has paid BILLIONS of DOLLARS to the Indians, and have aided them in many other ways!

The writing's on the wall. The pictures, and other evidence, reveal that no one has suffered more of a ghastly-atrocity than the Blacks that were kidnapped from the shores of Africa, and bought as Slaves! And, in spite of the horrendous-murderous-adventure of SLAVERY, neither our Ancestors, nor their offspring, have ever been paid one red penny! And I repeat, we are owed reparations, just like all other people that were paid reparations due to being wronged by another Government!

I am aware that there are some whom will argue against this truth, but their argument certainly will not change the truth. Accordingly, I have learned that some people love living in a state of denial! My suggestion is for them to take off their rose-colored glasses!

I am aware that some Black people have a job, work, and are paid, but it is all work and low pay for the majority. And once they have finished paying bills: rent, gas, lights, water, car note, home insurance, family insurance, car insurance, and buy a little food, you are broke again, and this is a continued cycle. To sum it up in a nutshell, the money that you make, goes right back to the Neo-Slave-Masters. There you are, working hard, but you don't own anything! Even the house, once you have completed paying for it, you still don't own it, because now you must pay taxes! And if you don't pay your taxes, the Government will, without a doubt, take the house!

The land is fifty seven million two hundred fifty five thousand square miles. Moreover, the land was here long before the Government, and that number proves that there's enough land for everyone to have a piece to enjoy. So why are the people having to pay taxes for land? The water is one hundred thirty nine million six hundred eighty five thousand square miles, and the water was here long before the Government. So why are the people having to pay for water?

Message to BlackMale Teenz -N- America

Black People, it is of paramount importance for you to teach your children and grandchildren about the horrors of Chattel Slavery, and the present horrors of Neo-Slavery! Consequently, the drive for REPARATIONS should never end until the offspring of the Black People that were kidnapped from the shores of Africa are fully, and completely compensated!!! I don't wear rose-colored glasses, so I know, without a doubt, that we are now living in the days of Neo-Slavery!

Remember, during Chattel Slavery, it was prohibited for the Slaves to be taught to read. The penalty was death. It is also a fact, that reading opens up the mind, and will make you knowledgeable of things that you should know, and today there is no penalty for reading. So please, start teaching your child/children to read at a young age, and that way, the older they get, the more they will enjoy reading. I believe that reading the right materials will help bring an end to the senseless murders between the teenage Black Males.

REPARATIONS! REPARATIONS!! REPARATIONS!!!

Chapter 16
Unity

Unity is more precious than silver and gold, and it is an ingredient that communities need, especially for the children's sake. You see, when families are Unified, it establishes a bilateral relationship with the community. This enables the children to communicate, play together, and be at peace and harmony. On the contrary, the absence of this bilateral relationship can, and will sometimes, cause some children to become bitter and angry. This sometimes causes them to act without due deliberation in a violent way.

When I was growing up, unity was deeply ingrained in the community, so that bilateral relationship was forever present. There were times when a family didn't have much to eat, and other families, including mine, would cook extra food and take it over, or the families would take turns inviting them over for dinner, or just went out and bought them some food. There were other kind acts that the people did for one another. You could always find

Message to BlackMale Teenz -N- America

someone that would let a person who was short on cash borrow what he/she needed. If one didn't have a car, or if his car was temporarily inoperative, there was someone that was always willing to give a ride.

But in today's society Black People have lost their way. In a lot of cases neighbors don't even speak, so the idea of someone feeding you when you are hungry, giving you a ride, letting you borrow some money, or giving you a place to lay your head temporarily, is all a pipedream! A lot of Black people today act upper class, because they have a little more than the people that they left behind in the ghetto! As opposed to lending a hand to help the people they left behind, they choose to pretend like they never knew those people.

It is undisputed that everyone's son can't become a pro football, basketball, golf, or baseball player. Neither a songwriter, film maker, music producer, actor, singer, movie producer, boxer, news or sports commentator, or land some other job that pays hundreds of thousands, or millions. And believe it or not, but some of the people as aforementioned, have went so far as to dis-associate themselves with their brothers, and sisters, and even their father. Please note, that I only wrote the above scenario to show a deeper picture. Moreover, people don't have to be rich to help each other.

Black people of today have become alienated, and in doing so they have put themselves in prison in their own house. It is sad that the children next door, across the street, and just a few houses down the street, can't play together and visit with each other. Yes, this is how it is today because the community is dichotomized. And therefore there is no bilateral relationship!

Black people, we need desperately to return to our roots. Moreover, it is a tangible fact, that: UNITED WE STAND, and divided we will undoubtedly FALL! I have a question. Why should we want to perpetuate the fall, when we now are aware of the disaster, misadventure, and the catastrophe of the fall?! Well, are we gonna continue on in the path of destruction, derived from division, or are we gonna do what is wise, and that is REUNITE?!

I am inclined to believe that if the Black communities will reunite, it will greatly aid in stopping the senseless murders of too many to be counted yearly, of the Black teenage males. Moreover, unity of the community brings back the bilateral relationship. The bilateral relationship moves a teenage murder from solely being a family issue, to making it a community issue!

So on that note, Black People: TO HELP Save the Children, let's REUNITE!!!

Chapter 17
Save the Children

I must profess that saving the children is momentous, and of the highest degree of importance, and it is unavoidable, because the children are indeed our future! Moreover, without our Black Children, there is certainly no future for Black People here in Amerika. I don't know of any other race on the planet that doesn't safeguard and protect their children, because they are aware of the fact that the children are their tomorrow. They also know, without a shadow of a doubt, that they don't want to be erased from the Planet Earth. I submit to you that if Blacks in Amerika don't undergo Consciousness-Raising in order to raise themselves to a living perpendicular so they can execute what it takes to Save The Black Youths, particularly the Black Male Youths, then I believe that in the next twenty years in Amerika, Every Black male youth will be in a plantation-prison, neoslavery camp, or an unwarranted, early grave!!!

During the Vietnam War, which was in a real war zone and over a nine year period, approximately twelve thousand Blacks lost their lives. But here in Amerika, and I want to quote the exact words that I heard one man that had done the math say, he stressed that every year, or every two years, that approximately twelve thousand or more Black male youths lose their lives to Black on Black crimes. That is indeed a staggering and shocking tragedy!

The aforementioned remonstrates two important features. First, it shows that it would be much safer for the Black male child to grow up in a real war zone, as opposed to the streets of Amerika. Secondly, it shows without a doubt, to those of us that have taken a bird's eye view of the matter, that the Black male child in Amerika is indeed an endangered species! The result of a Korrupt-Klandestine-Konspiracy! You see, without the Black male youths, there can be no reproduction of the Black Race!!!

Within the average Black household is a single parent, which mostly consists of the woman! Moreover, a child/children needs both parents! I submit to you that nature never designed it to be a one parent thing to raise the children, and it is not nature's design for families to divide. Premonition makes it clear that it is important for the Black people in Amerika to go back to the ways of our Ancestors! When the parents, grandparents, other relatives, and the community all took pride in raising the children.

Surely those that know can attest that the children had love and respect for their elders. They had love and respect for self, and kind. They had love and respect for their parents and grandparents;

and they would listen to what their parents, grandparents, and the elderly had to say. Consequently, the mothers and grandmothers weren't always crying like those of today, because of murder among the Black male youths! And the Black male youths weren't calling each other nigga/nigger all day and all night.

Black people, please put aside that foolish pride, and remember that United We Stand! Let us pledge to Stand United to Save the Black Youths! Because, without a doubt, THE CHILDREN ARE OUR FUTURE!!!

Chapter 18
Loving Everybody

Black people, for the most part, love teaching their children to love everybody, but they fail to teach their child/children to love self first, then to love their people! So the child/children grow up saying, "I love everybody", but never mention that he/she loves self. Through study and research I have learned that Nature never intended for anyone to love everybody. Therefore, it goes against all logic and reason for anyone to conceive that he/she has a duty to love everyone!

I submit to you that everything in creation has something that it hates! Do you think those African gazelles love those African lions and hyenas that run them down and eat them? Do you think that the small fish love the big fish that eat them? Do you think that our Ancestors loved the people whom kidnapped them, and then, during the times when the ships were over-loaded threw some of them overboard to be eaten alive by merciless sharks?! Do you think an innocent man who was sent to death row loves the police, D.A., judge, and jury whom sent him there? Do you think that he loved the Governor whom signed the death warrant for him to be murdered, and the prison guard whom pulled the switch? Please don't act without due deliberation, because I want you to thoroughly think about what I have written.

I have another testimony. GOD doesn't love everybody, and GOD never told anyone to love everybody! I am sure that many people will disagree with me on that, but that won't change the fact that it is true! Didn't GOD destroy Sodom and Gomorrah?! Accordingly, GOD certainly doesn't love the DEVIL and the DEVIL'S PEOPLE!!! GOD only LOVES THE PEOPLE whom are GODLY!!! I have learned that some wicked, evil, and DEVILISH PEOPLE got together and conspired to tell a lie on GOD when they said that GOD said to love everybody! Believe me, GOD never said that!

Please ponder this: How can you love everybody, when you don't know everybody? Since no one knows everybody, it would be, and is, mathematically impossible for anyone to love everybody.

The Bible, Leviticus, chapter 20, and the Lord spoke unto Moses, saying. Verse 9, For everyone that curseth his father or his mother shall be surely put to death: he hath cursed his father or his mother; his blood shall be upon him. Verse 10, And that man that committeth adultery with another man's wife, even he that committeth adultery with his neighbor's wife, the adulterer and the adulteress shall surely be put to death. Verse 11, And the man that lieth with his father's wife hath uncovered his father's nakedness: both of them shall surely be put to death; their blood shall be upon them.

Verse 12, And if a man lieth with his daughter in law, both of them shall surely be put to death: they have wrought confusion; their blood shall be upon them. Verse 13, If a man also lie with mankind, as he lieth with a woman, both of them have committed an abomination: they shall surely be put to death; their blood shall be upon them. Verse 14, And if a man takes a wife and her mother, it is wickedness: they shall be burnt with fire, both he and they; that there be no wickedness among them.

Verse 15, And if a man lie with a beast, he shall surely be put to death: and ye shall slay the beast. Verse 16, And if a woman approach unto any beast, and lie down thereto, thou shall kill the woman, and the beast: they shall surely be put to death; their blood shall be upon them.

Ecclesiastes, Chapter 3, To everything there is a season, and a time to every purpose under the heavens: Verse 8, A time to love, and a time to hate. . . I am going to stop there, because in my mind, the aforementioned verses from the Bible clearly prove my point that GOD doesn't love everybody, and that GOD never told anyone to love everybody. It also proves that there is a time to hate! I repeat that everything in creation has something that it hates!

I am not trying to copy anyone, but I have said the following on numerous occasions, "The mind is a terrible thing to waste!" I said that to say this: Black People, you must start reading more! You see, reading opens up the mind! The more you read, the more you will learn things that you never knew. Some will amaze, and some will undoubtedly shock the mind.

Lastly, Black People, first learn to love yourself. Teach the child/children to love self first! And if you feel the need to love someone else, make sure the love is bilateral and equal!!!

Chapter 19

The Greatest Love of All

It is important for Black parents to start teaching their child/children to love self first! You see, it is within Nature's design that loving self comes first, and when one learns to love him/herself first, than that is the greatest love of all!!! Once that type of love is manifested, the person then learns to respect and love others of the same kind.

Black on Black crime is at an all time high. Young Black males are, with malice, murdering each other! That is derived from the lack of respect and love for self, because surely if there were respect and love for self, they wouldn't find it convenient to murder each other the way that they do?! In my mind, the way they murder each other yearly, in large numbers, is like they perceived that it was only the killing of a fly or gnat.

One way to acknowledge the lack of respect and love among them, is the way that they call each other nigga or nigger all day and night, and in the presence of strangers and everyone else.

The word nigga or nigger is indeed a demeaning term. To use it so frequently the way they do only shows that they have a very low vocabulary, and hate for each other! I have even heard some say: I am a real nigga or nigger!" Well, I have yet to meet a real nigga or nigger.

It is a fact that Caucasians, Asians, nor Hispanics find it convenient to call each other foul names all day and night. Neither do other races of people. This madness among the teen Blacks has to stop!

There's something that I have noticed about teen Black males, when they communicate with other races, they don't call them nigga or nigger. They refer to that person by his birth name. That shows that they have no respect for self or kind, but have the utmost respect for others!

Singer Marvin Gaye said in one of his songs that: For only Love can conquer Hate! Singer George Benson said in one of his songs that: Learning to Love yourself is the Greatest Love of All! They are both absolutely correct!!! No respectable and intelligent people call each other foul names all day and night. Teen Black males, you cannot justify using that word all day and night. I don't care how you spell it, it is a demeaning word!

I say that it is important for the Black race to go back to the ways of our Ancestors! Back when the parents, grandparents, and other relatives, and the community raised the children. Moreover, during those days, there was self respect, and love, for self and kind, and it was overflowing!!! That is the way that it should be right now.

Young Black Brothers, is it so hard for you to say: peace by brother, or how are you doing my brother, to your fellow teen Black Brother, or to call him by his birth name? Moreover, that will be the right thing to do!!! Think about it.

Chapter 20
Baby Land

Baby Land is a cemetery in the state of Tennessee! The reason it is named Baby Land, is because the cemetery is covered with Black baby boys, who were murdered before they reached their first birthday! Now isn't that sad, that none of the babies there lived long enough to see their first birthday! If you were ever in any doubt, you should believe me now that the teen Black males in Amerika are an endangered species, which is derived from a Korrupt, Klandestine, Konspiracy, that is in place to prevent the reproduction process of the Black Race. It is an undisputed fact that the elimination of the Black Man will bring the Black race to nothing, because reproduction cannot occur without the Black Male!

    Thoroughly think about this please! Thousands of teen Black Males senselessly murdering each other yearly! Thousands of teen Black males on drugs and alcohol! Then there's thousands of teen Black males that are homosexual! Then there are thousands of teen Black males that are already in prison-hell throughout Amerika, that are serving long sentences, and thousands are entering the system yearly! Then there are those dying from the police bullets, and other races of people's bullets! Then those that are dying from car accidents, cancer, heart-attack, strokes, and other means!

Now how long do you think it will be before the Black man is erased completely? Well, I believe within the next twenty (20) years, every Black man in Amerika will be in a plantation-hellhole-prison, or an unwarranted early grave!

That is the primary reason that they're in Baby Land, they weren't even allowed to GROW UP! They were eliminated before their very first birthday!!! Moreover, I will simply reiterate that the Black male teens in Amerika are an endangered species and are headed for extinction!!! Please wake-up now, before it is too late!!!

Chapter 21
Destroy the Black Male Child by Any Means Necessary

The Black male child is an endangered species and is quickly headed for extinction. There are evil and wicked forces that are out to murder the Black male baby before his first birthday. Remember the cemetery known as Baby Land. Then there are those who are out to murder the Black male baby while he is still in his mother's womb, abortion doctors!!!

That is the primary reason for Abortion Clinics. They should change the name to: Baby Slaughter Clinics. Most doctors are clever and through the word game they trick women to surrender to an abortion. Looking back to when I was growing up, if the parents or parent could not adequately raise the child/children, the grandparents, Uncle and Auntie, or some other relative would be delighted to adopt or take part in raising the child/children.

Not in this day, the key word is abortion, and most women, especially Black women, will rush to have an abortion without thinking of the circumstances, and without discussing it with parents, grandparents, and even her husband, or if not married, her boyfriend. The sad part is the baby didn't ask to be conceived, and he doesn't have any say in the matter. No opportunity to take his case before a judge, jury, or anyone else. His only choice is to suffer a cruel and painful death!!!

Are you aware of the fact that during the murder, the doctor sticks a needle into the baby's head, and sucks out his brain? In the course of pulling the baby from the womb, the baby is so fragile, that the head, arm, fingers, and leg sometimes come off! Yet the doctor isn't charged with murder!!!

The United States Supreme Kourt in Washington, DC, in the case of Roe VS Wade, in 1973, legalized abortion, and that is the reason that the doctor is not charged with murder. The High Kourt has endorsed that sick, and Satanic way of murdering babies! Accordingly, since the case of Roe VS Wade in 1973, where the High Kourt legalized the murder of innocent babies, I have learned that approximately forty million (40,000,000) babies have been murdered, and that the majority of them are, of course, Black Babies!!!

I concede that the Korrupt-Klandestine-Konspiracy to erase the Black Race is no longer hidden! It is out in the open! If you still say that you don't see it, please take off your rose-colored glasses, because the Black male child's life is in danger! That is just the truth, although I am well aware that some people just can't handle the truth, but there is only One Truth, and the Truth is Universal, and the Truth can only be told one way!

I often wonder how can Amerika be called a Religious Nation when MURDER is the order of the day! That is from the top officials, to the bottom officials. Doesn't the BIBLE say that GOD says, "Thy shall not KILL"? When people don't care about INNOCENT BABIES, they don't care about anything, not even GOD's WORDS!!! Moreover, those people have got to be faceless, wicked, and evil! To sum it up in a nutshell, those PEOPLE HAVE TO BE DEVILS!!!

FOR GOD'S SAKE, PLEASE STOP IMMEDIATELY MURDERING INNOCENT BLACK BABIES!!! WILL THOSE WORDS MAKE A DIFFERENCE? I DOUBT IT!!!

Chapter 22
Trayvon Martin Part 1

Living in Amerika, a dog has more rights than a Black child! Here again, the RACIST system has refused to bring to justice, a White man for murdering a Black Child! It reminds me of the story that I read on Emmitt Till, a 14 year old Black child that was murdered in 1955 by a gang of White men for allegedly whistling at a White woman! Since the sixteen hundreds, seventeen hundreds, eighteen hundreds, the early nineteen hundreds, and to today's present, nothing much has changed for Black People in Amerika!!!

I say that dog fighting didn't start with Michael Vick, and to my knowledge, the evidence remonstrated that Michael Vick was never on the compound. In spite of that fact, the authorities rushed and indicted him, convicted him, and put him in prison!

But here in the case of Trayvon Martin, a Black child, whom was ferociously murdered solely because of his Back Skin, which also makes it a HATE CRIME, the authorities, both Federal and State, are nonchalant. They have therefore refused to bring that pernicious murderer of Trayvon Martin to JUSTICE! Even if a trial is convened, I am inclined to believe that he will not get convicted in Sanford, Florida!

The murderer even made mockery to Trayvon's parents while in the courtroom. He issued an artificially produced so-called apology, when he should have just kept his mouth closed. Accordingly, there are no words that he can stress that will justify, or bring any relief to Trayvon's parents for fiercely murdering their son solely because he was BLACK!!!

I want to know how many more children like Trayvon, and Emmitt Till are gonna have to be murdered before the parents, grandparents, other relatives, friends, and others are gonna say that enough is enough? Stop telling the children that everything is alright, or not so bad after all, when you know that is not true. Let the Black male child know that he has a wicked and evil open enemy that is waiting in the daylight and the nightlight to murder him!!!

Also let him know that that enemy is heartless, faceless, and merciless, and that he profoundly hates him exclusively for the color of his BLACK SKIN!!! Consequently, don't tell it to him one day, tell it to him every day, because to that enemy, his (the Black male child's) life isn't worth a thin dime. Let him know that the authorities are in active-consort with that enemy, so that enemy won't go to prison!

Black male children, please Beware! Here in the New Millennium in Amerika, a dog has more rights than you, and you will be sent to prison even if you didn't kill the dog!!! Trayvon Martin's confessed killer has yet to be brought to justice! Moreover, will he ever be brought to JUSTICE? I doubt it!!! This is indeed a sad, sad, day.

Chapter 23
Trayvon Martin Part 2

Let me reiterate to make things crystal clear, a dog has more rights in Amerika than a Black child. Actually, dogs belong in the wild, they are carnivorous and enjoy eating raw meat with blood running from it, just like other wild animals!!! Moreover, that is why a dog attack on a human is commonplace, they love the smell and taste of blood! I'm sure that some people are unwitting that the DOG is the offspring of the JACKAL and the WOLF! That is not guess work, but a scientific fact.

    Notwithstanding the aforementioned, there are some that wholly believe that the dog can be domesticated, until the damn carnivorous and vicious dog turns on him, her, or their child. I must profess that I have never owned a damn dog. I once had a puppy and a snake bit him and he died. I never thought about getting another one. I never thought about getting another one, because I became angry by being attacked by dogs when some of my friends and I rode our bicycle through certain communities, and I recall a couple of friends being bitten.

The gist of what I am saying is Trayvon Martin, a 17 year old Black child, was arbitrarily singled out solely because of his Black skin and for apparently walking through an aristocratic White neighborhood. There is no doubt in my mind that Trayvon would still be alive if he was White! Also, Trayvon would still be alive had that bringer of death, evil villain, stayed in the car as he had been told to do by the police dispatcher.

Now, once he disobeyed the dispatcher and got out of the car, he was acting from malice aforethought to murder Trayvon, just as he did!!! It is also undisputed that Trayvon had a cup of tea and a bag of skittles in his hand. Surely he was not going out to commit a crime with those items. Notwithstanding the aforementioned, the chief of police, acting with a deep-seated hate and prejudice for Blacks, refused to arrest the black-hearted, evil villain that spitefully murdered Trayvon, apparently because the attacker is Caucasian!!! On the contrary, if Trayvon had killed the Caucasian, the chief would not have hesitated to arrest Trayvon, and charge him with malice murder, even if it would've been self-defense! Also, Trayvon would've been denied bond!

Then the klanpig, fascist judge gave the murderer a bond for only 150,000 dollars. In other words, that was saying congratulations, now go out and murder another Black child, and this time, don't let anyone else see you! Please don't be misleading by the District Attorney's façade, in asking that bond be denied.

You see, you have to understand that those people are all wicked-devils and they do whatever it takes to trick the masses of the people. So for the most part, they always act in joint-concert. Moreover, had the D.A. found the judge's actions outrageously unethical, the D.A. had the right to appeal to the Florida Supreme Kourt.

The White mainstream news media is endeavoring to paint a picture of Trayvon as being the aggressor. I want to know what does his height and weight have to do with him being murdered? I believe those media of demons stressed that he was 5'11" and 150 lbs.. Actually, 150 lbs. is small for that height, and why would Trayvon try to be the aggressor in the face of a car, and a gun that shoots nine times? The malignant-hearted media never mentioned that the faceless, and unmerciful murderer of Trayvon actually weighs more than Trayvon, and that he violated the rules of engagement when he disobeyed the dispatcher and got out of the car.

Due to the aforementioned, he should be charged with malice murder, in the first degree, and therefore stripped of any stand your ground racist law! On the contrary, there are numerous people sending money to the malefactor to aid him with his defense. Now ain't that a bitch? While Trayvon's family suffers from the loss of their precious son! Surely that kind of egregious action aggrandizes their suffering. Those are the people whom need to ask themselves, would it be a joy to them if their child is maliciously murdered exclusively for the color of his SKIN???

Chapter 24
Florida

The State of Florida is the same State where just a few years ago, the wicked, evil, and racist District Attorney, got the new-lynch-mob Grand Jury to return a true bill of indictment against a twelve year old Black male child for allegedly malice murder. To my knowledge, this is what happened.

The male child was playing/wrestling with a six year old female child. Due to an unfortunate accident, the six year old child died. Moreover, there is never any doubt that it is sad and painful whenever a child is killed, and I can imagine the hurt that it take the family through.

The District Attorney was well aware that that was not a case of malice murder, but rather an unfortunate accident. Anyway, the child was tried, found guilty, and sentenced to life imprisonment. I salute the child's mother for her unconditional love and support. She fought until he was released from prison.

Paul J Austin

To my knowledge, there has been a few professional wrestlers accidentally killed in the ring, and throughout the history of sports, there have been other killings, and no one was charged with malice murder. But here we have a confessed mad-dog-killer, who murdered a seventeen year old, unarmed Black child, Trayvon Martin, and this same State of Florida has refused to bring the mad-dog-killer to justice. In my mind, the reason for the refusal is the mad-dog-killer is Caucasian/White. That's right; the situation is undoubtedly racially motivated.

Black male teens, this should serve as an eye-opener for you. You should now clearly see that the so-called justice system doesn't care about you! But, oh yes, they love every minute of the Black-on-Black crime of murder that you all so boldly have going on. Thousands of senseless and unjustified murders yearly, carried out by one teen brother to the other teen brother. I repeat, the time has come for you all to stop this madness of senseless murders and other crimes!

There are a lot of people, to include some Black people, that want to see all violent prone Black male teens disappear from the Planet Earth. The people feel that way because of what you all are doing. They see that you all don't have any respect, nor regard, for the value of precious life!!! I will say this, you all had better start reading a book that will open up your mind to the real reality of what's going on, unless you all have chosen the path to only be on this Planet a few more short years! EITHER WAY, THE MADNESS MUST STOP! THE MADNESS WILL STOP!!!

Message to BlackMale Teenz -N- America

Paul J Austin

Chapter 25
Rap Music

In the beginning rap music was clean, and some of the lyrics had profound massages. I particularly enjoyed Grand Master Flash, Sista Souljah, and Curtis Blow, and if my memory is serving me correctly, Sista Souljah was attacked by the Powers to be and her music was subsequently banned, in spite of the fact that her music was overflowing with true and profound messages. It was indeed a wake-up call to Blacks in Amerika. One of my favored songs by the Beloved Sista Souljah is: Slavery is Back in Effect!!!

Today's rap music is a profound disgrace! The lyrics are laced with distasteful and demeaning words. All you hear is nigga, nigga, nigga, kill a nigga, drive by, I hate niggas, bitch, and whore. Since they see every Black woman as a bitch or a whore, I want to ask all of them which one they see their mother and grandmother as.

Those faceless and evil minded idiots have made an enormous contribution to glorifying and magnifying the word nigga-nigger! They have also tremendously contributed to almost the eradication of a whole GENERATION OF BLACK YOUTHS, Black males particularly!!! The people who are speaking against that wicked rap music voices are not being heard, because the mainstream news-media isn't giving them any air-play! They have cut them off from all angles so as to have it appear that the Black population is in agreement with that evil music! When in fact, mass numbers of Blacks are in discord with that negative rap music!

Each of those wicked, evil, and negative rappers needs to be arrested, and charged with conspiracy to commit murder, or accessory to murder! I am aware that some people will disagree with me on that, and will probably say that no one is forcing the Black youths to go out and buy that brand of music. Well, that may be true, but the same can be said, and acknowledged, that no one is forcing the drug addict to go purchase drugs from the Drug Dealer, but the Drug Dealer still gets arrested, charged, and sent to prison! The same should apply to those Rappers!!!

I remember when comedian Richard Pryor frequently used the word NIGGER in all of his materials, on stage and albums. Mr. Pryor was never a stupid-fool! The man was extremely intelligent, and some of his materials had some true messages. Anyway, Mr. Pryor took a trip to Mother Africa, and it was there that he learned that the people in Africa DO NOT call each other NIGGER!!! Upon his return to Amerika, Mr. Pryor pledged allegiance to never again use the word NIGGER in any of his stage and album materials, and he honored his words.

Likewise, those Rappers of negative lyrics need to do as Mr. Pryor, and forthwith terminate using the word NIGGA, and all of the other defamed words that they love to use in their lyrics, or be forced to do so! The people need to hold mass protests and boycott their music. They are getting rich and richer off of the backs of dead children!!!

It is common knowledge that music plays a significant role in the way people think and act. When I was growing up the music was joyful. It made you get out on the dance floor and exhaust yourself with your woman. The love songs were there for you to hold her tight while slow dancing, and for you all to hurry home and try to make a baby. Some folks even called it baby making music.

During those days I never would've fathomed in a million years that our Ancestor's Heritage in music would be what it is today. Today's music, known as rap, has the Black youths, especially the Black males, hating self and each other, calling each other Nigga, and murdering each other by the thousands yearly! Moreover, those malignant-hearted, and black-hearted, rappers of that evil and distasteful rap music don't care anything about the Black Youths or Black People in general. Their thing is that dollar bill! In other words, they have been bought off; they have sold their soul to the Devil!!! It is time for you Black youths to wake-up, and stop buying that wicked and diabolical music! They are getting RICH off of your Blood!

Please note, I was informed by a Brother whom told me that that Caucasian/White rapper, and I don't remember his name, he stressed that he has sold more albums and is more popular, and has made more money, than any of those Black rappers. Now comes the interesting part. Consequently, he stated the Caucasian/White rapper did not degrade, nor demean, his Race in his lyrics!!!

Now that should prove, beyond a shadow of a doubt, that those Black rappers did not have to defame and degrade Black People with their evil lyrics! Black youths, I repeat, for God's sake stop buying their rap music!!!

Chapter 26
The Athlete

Black children are just as intelligent and superior in mind as all other children of the World. Therefore, when they finish high school and go off to college, they should seek to become a doctor, physicist, scientist, archaeologist, architect, psychologist, psychiatrist, professor, engineer, or to seek a higher learning in some other field, not just endeavor to become an athlete!!! Moreover, the parents and grandparents, for the most part, must encourage them to do this.

I concede that our Ancestors did not endeavor to become an athlete. A lot of our Ancestors had great and superior minds, and this was long before the hieroglyphics! Our Ancestors had built great civilizations!!! The mind is a terrible thing to waste! You see, there are some people that have great athletic ability, but everyone doesn't get picked. As a matter of fact, the inventors never intended for everyone to get picked! Consequently, having great athletic ability is in reality, a minute and trivial matter.

The aforementioned educational fields manifest the people that make a significant contribution in this world that we live in. In my mind, a carpenter, brick mason, and electrician is more important than an athlete! If it wasn't for those skills of people, we certainly wouldn't have a place to lay our head. Accordingly, I will admit that some athletes make a lot of money, but I will also admit that athletes do not make any significant contributions to the world.

Please, Black People, stop telling your young son to be like Mike, or any of those other renowned athletes. Some of you even have your daughters wanting to be like Mike. Consequently, athletes are not role models! Therefore, they should not be acknowledged as role models. I am sure that some of you will disagree with me, but that won't change the truth of the matter.

I have read and studied about the life and times of the beforehand people. They are certainly role models, and people that Black children should endeavor to be like, or at least carry on in their works; Mahatma Gandhi, Marcus Garvey, Elijah Muhammad, Steven Biko, Noel Drew Ali, Medgar Evers, Frederick Douglass, Denmark Vessey, Nat Turner, Malcolm X, Dr. Martin Luther King Jr., Harriet Tubman, Ida B. Wells, Sojourner Truth, Winnie Mandela, Rosa Parks, Assata Shakeer, Mark Clark, Fred Hampton, and Stokeley Carmichael! Those names are just a few!

I am aware that some people will argue that some of those people were about violence, but I will whole-heartedly disagree, because those people were superior-minded and intelligent. They loved themselves and their Black people. For the most part their fight was/is for freedom, justice, equality, social, political, and economic emancipation for the masses of the Black People in Amerika, who are the downtrodden, and disenfranchised!!!

I am also aware that Mahatma Gandhi, Steven Biko, and Winnie Mandela's fight was not for the emancipation and liberation for Blacks in Amerika, but they wanted justice for their people as well! People whom were being oppressed and persecuted by another people. Also, to my knowledge, Ms. Assata Shakur, and Ms. Winnie Mandela are still alive.

We as a people don't need any more athletes. So please no more athletes. Consequently, rise up Black youths in Amerika, and show the World just how great you are!

Chapter 27
Dead Man Walking, Part 1

The dead man walking is a mentally dead person. He is that person that doesn't have any knowledge, wisdom, or understanding. Therefore, he doesn't have the slightest clue as to what is really going on in this World in which we live in today. Moreover, the Black male teens in Amerika have almost become the embodiment of the dead man walking! I must profess that it is sad, because we are now living in the information age.

The Black male teens believe it to be a badge of honor to be functioning stupid and illiterate. Consequently, functioning in those two categories is what makes them disagreeable and easily angered. That is the main reason that they don't hesitate to murder each other as they do. You see, when a person is functioning stupid and illiterate he doesn't have the main ingredients of logic and rational, so nine times out of ten he is going to elect to murder another Black male teen. In doing so, he is only murdering himself as well, but he hasn't come to realize that.

Paul J Austin

Black male teens in Amerika, it is time for you to come to know that your life is in an impending danger! In order for you to know that that is an undisputed fact: YOU MUST START READING THE RIGHT BOOKS!!! I'm referring to the kind of books that will raise you out of your sleeping death state. You see, there is a pernicious spreading evil, and it is a group of people. They are the ones that put together the Korrupt-Klandestine-Konspiracy to remove the Black man from all parts of Amerika altogether. Moreover, this is not a video-game! This is real!!!

Black male teens murdering each other yearly by the thousands are, without a doubt, aiding the Konspirators. The guns that you all are murdering each other with are like child's play when it comes to the weapons that they have which are going to be used to uproot and erase you all altogether! This is why you all must start educating yourselves right now, so that you can escape the great disaster and catastrophe that is, without a doubt, coming to visit you soon!

Reading takes you to new dimensions. Reading takes you out of that box of darkness, and brings you into the light, so that you can think and know. Reading takes that blindfold off of your eyes, and enables you to see the real picture. You will then know that everything is not alright!!! I have carried out a lot of reading, studying, and investigations and I still do! Man should seek knowledge, from the cradle to the grave! Anyway, I am disabused, and what I mean by that is, my eyes are wide opened, so I am no longer a dead man walking! Please note that what I see, and know, is not a pretty picture. A pernicious and pestilent danger is coming soon!!!

Consequently, what I am saying is no longer a secret. It is now out in the open. It is the Korrupt-Klandestine-Konspiracy to subvert the Black man! In order to know that, and to clearly understand that, you gotta have correct knowledge, and a lot of knowledge is derived from reading! Black male teens, I submit to you, that in this day and hour, it is too dangerous to be walking around in triple stages of darkness!!!

PLEASE WAKE-UP NOW, BEFORE IT IS TOO LATE!!! The beforehand are some books that I suggest that you read, study, and investigate, then take a look around: Message to the Blackman in America, The Fall of America, The supreme Wisdom, and The Mother Plane, by Mr. Elijah Muhammad. The Unseen Hand, by Mr. Ralph Epperson. Behold A Pale Horse, by Mr. William Cooper. The Browder Files, by Mr. Tony Browder. From Niggas to Gods, I don't remember the author's name. Alice In Wonderland and the World Trade Center Disaster, The Biggest Secret, and The Truth Shall Set You Free, By Mr. David Icke. Those books will give you a start. There are many, many more.

Chapter 28
Dead Man Walking, Part 2

There is another dead man walking! Those are the ones that are trapped inside of those abysses of hellhole-plantation-prisons throughout the Amerika. While I was confined at Georgia State Prison in Reidsville, Georgia, a comrade of mine allowed me to read some important, and somewhat shocking, information that one of his brothers had sent him.

To the best of my knowledge, the information that I am about to share with you all reads in pertinent part: that in the event of Civil Unrest, or Civil Disobedience, that an Executive Order will be executed to murder all of the prisoners in county jails, State and County prisons throughout Amerika. The above order was almost issued during former President of the United States, Lyndon B. Johnson's tenure.

Black male teens, you are without the slightest hesitation, carrying out senseless murders yearly. You all are coming to prison by the thousands yearly, and with extremely long prison sentences.

On that note, you will be locked in, with nowhere to run to escape the DOOM that is coming your way. There is only one way to escape! You must stop the madness of those heinous and hideous crimes that you are committing. Therefore, you must be inclined to seek knowledge, which will give you wisdom and understanding. Consequently, you will then know, without a doubt, that destruction is coming, and you can then avoid it.

    I cannot propel you to get on the path of Constructive-Matters. I can only share with you what I have learned. You will come to know what you must accomplish once you obtain, read, and study the books that I have made you aware of in Chapter Twenty Seven. I say to you, what we have here is your salvation. Only you can make that decision to get on the Right path, or to stay on the Wrong path, and suffer the unavoidable doom of destruction that is coming soon.

Paul J Austin

Chapter 29
The Picture of Life

I want you to over-stand, and understand, that the picture of life is not a video game. The picture of life is real and the people are real. Therefore, I submit to you that everyone on the Planet Earth only have one life to live! We must learn to take advantage of that, and live the best possible life that we can. Moreover, we must also try to hold on to our precious life for as long as we can! That is what rational thinking people do, because they are aware that it is out of the realm of possibility, and mathematically impossible, to go out somewhere else and get another life after the one that we have is gone!!!

Black male teens, here in Amerika you all need to curtail the bringer of death type lifestyle that you have embarked upon. Start trying to live as long as you can, and the best that you can on this plane, where you know you have life. It is easy to die! Even if you miss the graveyard and are sent to a plantation-prison you still die, because you will be there forever, or for the best years of your life! That is just the uncut and unadulterated truth!!! I submit to you that only a super-stupid-fool will hasten himself to an early grave!

Our Ancestors surely did not rush to go to the graveyard. The Bible speaks on how some of them lived to be hundreds of years old. One is recorded as living the longest ever on Earth, and he was nine hundred sixty nine years old. I invite you to do a little research on that. Everyone at some point in time will come to know that he/she must die one day, but you don't have to rush to the graveyard.

The Bible, Job-Chapter 7, verse 9; As the cloud is consumed and vanisheth away: so he that goeth down to the grave shall come up no more. The Bible, Ecclesiastes-Chapter 9, verse 5; For the living know that they shall die; but the dead know not anything, neither have they any more a reward; for the memory of them is forgotten.

Black male teens, you have two choices. Number one, you can be recalcitrant, and stay on that road of destructive-matters, and end up in a plantation-prison, or an early grave. Consequently, when you die in your teens or early twenties, you are still just a new born baby. Number two, you can curtail the crime spree and vicious murders, get on the road to Constructive-Matters, and not only make your family, friends, and the elderly people in the community proud of you, but the whole world will give you a standing ovation. They will say: Thank God, The Sleeping Giant Has Awakened!!!

Chapter 30
Constitutional Rights

Let me make one thing perfectly clear: Blackmen, Blackwomen, and Blackchildren, here in Amerika we don't have any constitutional rights. Now, please allow me to paint an unclouded and clear picture as to what I am saying. According to the Korrupt and Wicked system, a person is innocent until proven guilty! Well, I hereby dispute that and I'm sure that many others will agree with me, because they are aware as I am that, that is one of the Biggest Lies that has ever been told! Moreover, you are guilty, guilty, guilty, until the diabolical and evil system decides to release you, and unfortunately many leave dead!!!

I submit to you that if we had constitutional rights, Mr. Troy Davis would still be alive. His case serves as a prime example! Mr. Davis was on death row here it two hundred years behind the times Georgia. He maintained his innocence from the first day on arrest. Consequently, there was never any concrete evidence, the only thing the State had, is what is called unreliable eye-witness testimony, where people sometimes believe that they saw something, then later realize that they were not sure as to what they saw. Anyway, seven of those nine witnesses later recanted their statement and testimony.

Now people, that was more than enough of a reason to stop the murder of Mr. Troy Davis. The Pope and Mr. Jimmy Carter, former United States President, and just too many other people to be counted, pleaded with those merciless, unmerciful, heartless, and faceless Georgia officials to not murder Troy. All of their entreaties were to no avail. You see, as opposed to releasing Troy, or at least giving him a new trial, the wicked and tyrannical system chose to murder him! With that type of ending they will never have to acknowledge that they had an innocent man on death row for several decades!

I repeat, Black People in Amerika do not have any constitutional rights. We never have, and we never will. That is just the uncut and unadulterated truth. We as a People must never forget that our Ancestors were shanghaied from Mother Africa, and brought here to be Slaves only! Accordingly, it was never intended for the Slaves, nor the offspring of the Slaves, to be equal to the Slave-Masters, nor the Slave-Masters' children! If you are disinclined to believe me, then just do a little research for yourself. The United States Supreme Court case of Dred Scott VS. Sanford 15 LED 691, 19 HOW 393, May 12, 1856, will put you on point as a start.

Let me also show the primary reason that we do not have any constitutional rights. You see, HUMAN RIGHTS come before constitutional rights, and I will simply reiterate, Black People in Amerika do not have any Human Rights! Again, when the Slave-Masters stripped our Ancestors of their Mother tongue, that murdered us! It took away the Right that is within Nature's design: Which is the Right for us to be recognized as Human Beings!!! Moreover, since we are not recognized as Human Beings, and not just in Amerika, but throughout the Whole World, we don't have any human rights, constitutional rights, civil rights, and any other rights!!!

Allow me to go a little further. Amerika is a multi-cultural society, but if you hear two people speaking the Chinese language, and you see that they are Chinese, then you will know that they are from China. If you hear two people speaking the Japanese language, and you see that they are Japanese, you are aware that they are from Japan. And likewise with other people, when you hear them talking, and if you can recognize them to be from a foreign land, whether it's France, Mexico, Russia, Puerto Rico, Italy, Philippines, Cuba, or some other country, you come to know where they are from, their home-base!

You see, it is the language that ties a person to a particular Country. Therefore, Black People in Amerika are not recognized as human beings, because we do not have a home-base, even though a lot of us are aware that our Ancestors were brought here from

Africa. Consequently, most of us are unaware as to what part of Africa our Ancestors were stolen from, and we certainly wouldn't recognize our Mother tongue if we heard it. So, in reality, we have been, and are, displaced!!! That is because when we hear each other speaking the English language, the English language is not our Mother tongue, so it certainly doesn't tie us back to any part of Mother Africa!!!

So, teen Black males, when you enter the Kourtroom thinking that you have some constitutional rights, you can discard that pipedream, because you don't even have any human rights! So the judge, District Attorney, and your so-called defense attorney, all see you as not being a human being! So you won't receive one penny worth of justice. Moreover, the justice that you will receive is injustice!!! Therefore, I suggest that you all stop, right now, committing those astronomical senseless murders each year and get on the track of Constructive-Matters!!! That is the only thing that can save you from the Unavoidable-Disastrous-Doom that's Coming Soon!!!

Please note, that Mr. Troy Davis is just one of hundreds that was sitting on death row in a hellhole-plantation-prison in Amerika, and was innocent! In spite of that fact, they were murdered! Don't misconstrue my writings, I am not about hate. I am just a lover of the truth. Therefore, I prefer Right, over Wrong! The time has come for the people to choose Right or Wrong, Good or Bad. Moreover, there isn't a multiple choice, so it is inevitable that you can choose only one!

Message to BlackMale Teenz -N- America

Chapter 31
Nigger! Nigga! Nigger! Nigga!

Nigger, Nigga, Nigger, Nigga, that's all I hear coming out of the mouths of young Black males! Nigger, Nigga, Nigger, Nigga, has become them! Nigger, Nigga, Nigger, Nigga, is the only word that they know. I am so tired of hearing the words Nigger, Nigga, Nigger, Nigga, that it makes me sick from the top of my head, to the bottom of my feet! Nigger, Nigga, Nigger, Nigga, is in their blood! Nigger, Nigga, Nigger, Nigga, is their brain! Hey Nigger! That's my Nigga! What's up Nigger?! Nigga!

The young Black males can't go anywhere without Nigger! When they get in a car there's Nigga! When he gets on the bus or train, there's Nigga! Nigga is his shadow! When he looks in the mirror, there's Nigger! When he sits down to eat, there's Nigga! When he picks up the phone, there's Nigger! Nigga even goes to the toilet with him, and when he goes to the shower, of course, nigger goes with him! His woman is Nigga! Before he goes to sleep at night, he hugs and kisses Nigger, and upon waking up the next morning and before he brushes his teeth! He hugs and kisses Nigga!

Nigger is always with him! Nigga don't want to let him go! Him and nigger have become inseparable! Nigga is the reason that he can't stay in school! Nigger is the reason why he can't get a job! Nigga is the reason why almost the whole world hates him! Nigger is the reason that he is so stupid and ignorant! Nigga is the reason why he has low self esteem! Nigger is the reason why he hates himself! Nigga is the reason why he hates his Black male teen Brother! Nigger is the reason why he walks around with his pants hanging down, and has no shame at showing the World his foul smelling buttocks! Nigga has, without a doubt, disgraced him!

Nigger is the reason why he doesn't take care of his children! Nigga is the reason why he sees every Black woman as a bitch or a whore! I can't help but wonder, does he see his mother and grandmother as a bitch or a whore?! The young Black males are so in love with nigger, he believes whole-heartedly that nigga is his best friend! He believes whole-heartedly that nigger will always be around! He believes whole=heartedly that nigga will never let him down! Nigger is the reason why he buys and listens to that meaningless, detestable, and repulsive rap music! Some say that he and nigga is married! Nigger is the reason why he chooses destructive matters! Nigga is the reason why he is so easily angered! Nigger is the reason why he acts without due deliberation! Nigga is his livelihood!

He can't function without nigger! Nigga manipulates him! Nigger even tricks him! Nigga has him thinking he is a man! He is so proud to be a nigger! He will stand on top of Mount Everest, which is twenty nine thousand one hundred forty one feet high, and tell the whole world that he is a nigga! He will kill anyone who will dare try to come between him and nigger! He believes the whole world revolves around him and nigga! Nigger is the reason why he can't think! Nigga is the reason why he chooses death over life. Nigger is the reason why he hates his Black Father! Nigga is the reason why he is on drugs and alcohol! He says that nobody better lay a finger on his nigger! Nigga is the reason why plantation-prisons, and the graveyard are his final destination! Nigger really hates him, but he is too narrow-minded to know it! Nigga is the primary reason that he dies so young!

Please listen carefully young Black males!!! The time has arrived for you all to stop calling each other nigger, nigga, nigger, nigga all day and all night! The time has arrived for you all to stop senselessly murdering each other yearly, by the thousands! Please listen to the voice of reason, and stop doing it right now! Moreover, if you refuse, you will be forced to stop!

Lastly, nigger is the reason why he murders his young Black Brother without the slightest hesitation! Nigga is the reason why he is shameless and calls the other one nigger, nigga, nigger, nigga in front of family, friends, and even strangers! Nigger has turned him into an uncivilized brute-beast! Nigga is his eyes! Nigger is his tongue! Nigga is his name! Nigger is all over him!

Nigga don't even like him! Nigger has got to go! Nigga is the reason why he believes that he is a filthy pig, but what he doesn't know is he is a King! I want to tell him, but I can't get past nigger! Yeah, nigga never goes to sleep!

Well, I am going to pray and ask God to visit him and tell him! Moreover, that won't work, because I heard some remarkably knowledgeable wise men say that God has already came to visit us, and that God found the man that He was looking for, and that God taught Him for three and a half years! It was also said that God has left and He won't be back! Brother, that is profoundly deep, and I didn't know that! Well, I can only hope that someone will get the message to him, to let him know that he is not a pig, but rather, a King! I hope so too, because it's a matter of LIFE or DEATH!!!

Nigger, Nigga, Nigger, Nigga is a repulsive word! Our Ancestors fought other races who would dare call them Nigger! Nigga! Nigger! Nigga! The R and B group known as Sly and the Family Stone once had a song out called: Don't Call Me Nigger/Whitey! I concede that if the word doesn't reach him in time so that he will know he is not a pig, but a King, in the hopes that he will start carrying out his duties as a King, Nigga is, without a doubt, going to BETRAY HIM! JUST AS JUDAS BETRAYED JESUS!

Chapter 32
Organizations

The NAACP; the ACLU; the Public Defenders; Centurion Ministries; The Innocence Project; and all of the others all have a common theme which says; we don't have the money, nor the resources to investigate you. Sorry we couldn't be of more help. That is a preposterous and monstrous joke. You see, for the most part, those organizations are not there to accommodate the innocent, nor to aid people that are being discriminated against. That slogan is all a façade!

I submit to you that the primary reasons for those organizations are to steal millions of dollars from the hard working taxpayers, through donations, and other ways. Consequently, they are there to tell mendacious-malicious lies to the population at large, to have the people thinking that they are there if you need them, and that their mission is to free the innocent people behind bars, among other things. That is why infrequently you will read an article, or hear on the news, or some show where an organization helped to free an innocent person. That is infrequently, and so far apart! That is why if you check the records you'll find that those organizations don't aid one percent of the innocent people behind bars!

In my mind, what that shows, and remonstrates, is that they are working in joint-concert with this tyrannical and totalitarian, injustice-judicial-system! Therefore, as long as those organizations can keep the masses of the people bamboozled and tricked into believing that they are there to serve the people, and are doing a wonderful and magnificent job, they can, and will, continue to live the sumptuous and lavish lifestyles that they are living, by stealing millions of dollars yearly from the hard working taxpayers without doing any work, or less than one percent of work to help those innocent prisoners!

Black male teens, I am well aware that that injustice-judicial-machine sends innocent people to prison without the slightest bit of hesitation. Therefore, I know without a doubt that some of you are innocent! I have seen countless cases where there were five arrested, and all were charged with malice murder, and there was one gun and shooter. Also, countless rape cases where there wasn't any DNA evidence, no finger prints, no positive identification, and no other concrete evidence, and in spite of that, a guilty verdict, and harsh sentence was handed down. The list goes on.

I believe in punishment for crime, but I also believe that the punishment must fit the crime. I also firmly believe that absolutely no innocent people should be in prison, but unfortunately, we are living in a society that frequently sends men, women, and children to prison and death row, that are actually INNOCENT!!! It is the order of the day! I had to point that out, because I want you to be aware that if you get sent to prison and are innocent, those organizations are not gonna lift one finger to help you!

Chapter 33
Korrupt-Klandestine-Konspiracy

I concede that there can be no reproduction of the Black Race without the Black man, and wicked and evil men are aware of the aforementioned. Moreover, there is a Korrupt-Klandestine-Konspiracy in place to remove the Black man from the planet altogether, and the primary target is the Black male teens!!! That is why every prison and jail throughout Amerika is overflowing with teenage Black males, even though Blacks only make up twelve percent of the Amerikan population.

Surely some will argue that the Black male teens are committing heinous and hideous crimes. Well, I won't try to dispute the truth, but on the contrary, that does not justify the Korrupt-Klandestine-Konspiracy! You see, the Blue-print to eradicate and destroy the Black man was already in place long before the Black male teens started committing unnecessary, gruesome crimes. I concede that the unnecessary, gruesome crimes that the Black male teens are committing are part of the Konspirators Blue-print!

I have a question that I would like for the readers to thoroughly think about. What is being done to prevent the senseless Black on Black murders in astronomical numbers yearly? I submit to you that absolutely nothing is being done to prevent those crimes. Consequently, a lot is being done to encourage the Black male teens to continue murdering each other yearly. In doing so, the Konspirators can try to justify the building of more prisons and jails, and tougher laws! However, the aforementioned is not the cure to the problem.

A lot of Black people are inclined to believe that the cure to the problem is to allow the Blacks in Amerika who are descendants of the Chattel Slaves to separate from Amerika, and establish their own Government!!! The voices say that that Government will not be a Wicked Government, but instead a Righteous Government! I have also learned that the Konspirators are actively working to prevent the establishment of a Government by the offspring of the Chattel Slaves.

The primary reason for that is as I have previously stressed, the Konspirators are out to erase, and remove the Black man from the planet earth altogether, and the Black male teen is the prime target! You all are the prime target, because the evil and wicked Konspirators are endeavoring to obstruct the future generations of the Black Race! Moreover, the Konspirators are well aware that you all (Black male teens) cannot make babies from the graveyard and plantation-prisons!!!

The Chinese, the Japanese, the Russians, the Germans, the Koreans, the Philippines, and the Italians, to name a few, all have their own Government. Therefore the descendants of the Chattel Slaves have a Universal Human Right to have their own Government! Don't you agree? I have also learned that the Konspirator's plan to impede the Children of the Chattel Slaves from having their own Government will surely fail!!!

Chapter 34

The Grand Jury

The District Attorney, after a person has been arrested, allegedly takes the matter before the grand jury with the endeavor to obtain an indictment. Moreover, the accused person, particularly ordinary citizens, is not allowed to attend those proceedings, so nine times out of ten, or ten times out of ten, the grand jury returns a true bill of indictment. This is wholly unfair, prejudicial, and discriminatory, because the District Attorney paints a one sided picture! Since the accused person isn't allowed at the grand jury proceedings to put forth evidence to dispute the District Attorney's malicious tactics of lies in a lot of cases, the grand jury believes his/her words are the unadulterated truth.

It is an undisputed fact that there are two sides to every story. So on that pertinent fact, the accused person should be allowed to be at the grand jury proceedings to tell his side of the story! Consequently, that discriminatory practice doesn't apply to legislators, law enforcement officials, judges, prosecutors, District

Attorneys, and others who are part of the Klandestine-Konspiracy to erase the Black man and Black male child from the planet altogether.

Here in the heart of the Dirty South, better known as Georgia, there is a popular belief among the people that are disabused, in other words, those who have knowledge, wisdom, and understand that seventy five percent of those true bill indictments are rubber stamped! What I mean by that is: those indictments have been fabricated by the District Attorney to have it appear that they were returned by the grand jury! Moreover, those indictments that are the product of fabrication are null and void, and the people that are in prison derived from those false indictments are being held illegally.

The above information should not be difficult to understand. Please think about the beforehand. If the judicial system was about justice, then surely the law would allow the accused person to attend the grand jury proceedings to dispute the theory by the District Attorney, which may cause the grand jury to return a no true bill! Since that is not the procedure, it leads those with supreme knowledge to believe that there is some foul-play! I have thoroughly analyzed the matter, and I believe, as many others, that there is some foul-play involved, because I cannot conceive any logical, nor justifiable reason to deny an accused person of a crime the right to appear before the grand jury, and present evidence to show that he is not the person who committed the crime.

The system is wholly and completely unfair. The primary design of the judicial system is to entrap the Black male teens, and put them in a plantation-prison for the best years of their lives, or for the remainder of their natural lives, in order to thwart and prevent the reproduction of the Black Race!!! The above writing is not pseudoscience, but rather a scientific and undisputed fact. Black male teens, please, Wake up before it is too late!!!

Chapter 35
The Jury

The law unequivocally states that a person accused of a crime has a fundamental constitutional right to have a trial by a fair and impartial jury. That right also allegedly extends to the right to a jury of one's peers. A lot of people, to include myself, can testify that Black people in Amerika don't have any constitutional rights, so the aforementioned doesn't apply to Black people! Moreover, in most cases, the jury is prejudiced and biased to the extreme when the accused person is Black, and in most cases the accused Black male is never tried by a jury of his peers, if ever!

The beforehand is undisputed that here in Way Down in Dixie Land, two hundred years behind the times Georgia, when the accused is a Black man, or Black male teen, the jury has a preconceived and arbitrary notion that he is guilty. Therefore, conviction is unavoidable, even in cases where there is not even one small piece of evidence to convict.

Paul J Austin

    The jury is almost never fair and impartial! The jury is not, as the system wants people to believe, rational fact-finders! I am aware that some people will oppose me, and say that what I have stressed is not true. Consequently, my words are based upon the undisputed fact that the jury sends innocent people to prison and to death row too often!!! You see, the people of the system are wicked and evil, and they maliciously designed the system to enable them to send innocent people to prison. Please note that the majority of innocent people in Amerika's plantation-prisons are Black males!

    I am only one of many people who are innocent and trapped in a hellhole plantation-prison and cannot get a minute amount of justice! That is because the only justice that a Black man receives in Amerika, is INJUSTICE!!! Notwithstanding the fact that I have served twenty nine years, and the jury didn't have one small piece of evidence to justify a conviction.

    A few years ago nine men were released from Chicago's death row, because further investigations and tangible evidence proved them to be innocent! The Governor stressed that he was appalled and shocked, so he put a halt on all further executions to carry out investigations to determine if anyone else was innocent. So surely the jury is not rational-fact-finders, when they return verdicts of guilty that send innocent people to death row!!! I am sure that we would be shocked if we knew the number of innocent people that were sent to death row, and have already been murdered!!! You would also be shocked if you knew the number of innocent people that are presently in prison and on death row. The numbers that are sent yearly, due to merciless, wicked juries!!!

The theme song in Amerika is a Black man, or Black male child did it, so the target for arrest and conviction is a Black man or Black male child, and that is only if the fierce and ferocious cops don't shoot you dead on the spot! Moreover, the jury is racist to the extreme, and that's what makes conviction inevitable. I am sure that some will argue and say that the matter is no longer discriminatory because there are Blacks on the jury. Well, I am aware that there are some people whom serve on the jury that are wrapped in Black, but they are better known as oreo-cookies, sold-out, sell-out, turncoats!!! Consequently, that description applies to the majority of them.

A lot of people hope and pray that the system will one day change, and start treating all people fair, and with equality, regardless of their skin color! Well, I am here to serve as a reminder, and therefore, I must tell you that the system will never change! Moreover, the system will never change, because the people of the system are wicked, evil, and pestilent, by their very nature!!! Therefore, they cannot change their murderous ways, even if they wanted to!!!

I must also stress, for those who may not know, that the only way Black people will receive FREEDOM, JUSTICE, and EQUALITY, is they must be under the guidance of a

RIGHTEOUS BLACK GOVERNMENT!!! That is just the unadulterated truth!!!

Chapter 36
Debt Never Paid

Amerika wants the whole world to believe that this is the most civilized country in the world. A lot of people can, and will, attest to the fact that that theory is as far away from the truth as the sun is from the earth, 93,000,000 miles away. Let me paint a clear picture on what I am saying. It doesn't matter if a person serves ten, twenty, thirty, or forty years in prison-hell, his debt is never paid.

You see, once released from prison-hell, he is still tied to the yoke of the new-slavery, which is derived from the new-colonialism. The term is called parole, and for the slightest violation here in Behindhand, Racist Georgia he is returned to prison. Even for the arrest of a traffic violation, or an arrest due to mistaken identity. Oh, and there's a flip side to the coin. Moreover, when he has been successfully released from parole, his debt is still never paid.

Consequently, his full, so-called rights are never restored. If he is arrested again, and accused of a new crime, during his trial the District Attorney makes known to the judge and jury the crime that he had served time for twenty or thirty years ago, or longer. This causes an already prejudice, bias, and hateful jury to return a verdict of guilty within a few minutes, without deliberations.

There are many countries that restore a person's full rights once he has served the time for the crime, and upon release there is no parole, nor probation. Also, if the person is arrested and tried again, his old case that he served time for is not revealed to the judge and jury. A lot of people are aware that the primary reason that this Amerikan system is so wicked and evil is derived from the fact that the people of the system are stuck on Chattel Slavery procedures, and they see all Black people in Amerika as Chattel Slaves, regardless of their status.

Chapter 37
Evil-minded Judges

There are only a few judges that will adhere to the law, and they are the ones that dole out sentences fairly to all, regardless of the color of the defendant's skin! On the contrary, ninety eight percent of all judges are malevolent, black-hearted, racist, and diabolical, and a Black defendant is over-sentenced every time he goes in front of a wicked judge. A prime example: I met a guy while at Georgia State Prison that received twenty five life sentences, and three hundred years. Now, it is mathematically impossible for him to serve that sentence, don't you agree?

Moreover, a lot of prisoners, upon meeting him initially, think that he has at least fifteen counts of murder! They become shocked to learn that he doesn't have one count of murder! A lot of people, to include myself, are aware that when a racist judge sentences a Black man to an over-kill sentence, he is making a clear statement that if it had been possible, he would have imposed the death sentence.

My case also serves as a prime example. John H. Land, chief judge, and better known as the hanging judge at that time, imposed an over-kill sentence on me, which is life imprisonment, but according to Georgia law O.C.G.A. 17-10-1 (a), the proper sentence is one to twenty years. The life penalty, according to Georgia law O.C.G.A. 17-10-7 (b), is the sentence for repeated offenders, whereas I am a first time offender! I am also innocent, and I never should have been arrested, or convicted.

Over the years I have filed at least four pleadings entitled: Motion to Correct Sentence, in the Superior Kourt of Muscogee County, all availed to nothing due to the evil-minded and racist judges that are over that Konsolidated Government District. Therefore I am forced to languish in a plantation-prison-hell, because I don't have the help and other resources needed to expose this extreme racially motivated injustice to the eyes of the public.

I concede that the wicked and evil players of this New-Slavery System are well aware that most Black males who are trapped in hell-plantation-prisons throughout the United States of Amerika don't have the money nor other resources needed to expose their injustice. The evil players are also aware that there is no UNITY, nor TRUST, among Black People! The term is better known as DIVIDE and CONQUER!!! Consequently, too many to be counted Blacks like Johnnie, as aforementioned with the over-kill-sentence of twenty five life sentences plus, must languish in hell-plantation-prisons for a long, long time, for some, until death takes over them.

The message in this book is for the most part aimed at the Black male teens, in hopes that they will adhere to the message, and carry out that which is necessary to circumvent and avoid the many traps that are out there to lead them to an unwarranted early grave, and to a hell-plantation-prison, where they will spend the best years of their lives! Really, a Sophisticated form of GENOCIDE, because you cannot make babies from plantation-prison. Moreover, the children are our future, and without the children, there can be no future!!!

I submit to you, that there are too many to be counted BLACKMALE TEENZ WITH OVERKILL SENTENCES!!! And the sad part, they are gonna die in a hellhole-plantation-prison if they don't get some help!!!

Chapter 38
News Media

    The racist and wicked people of the News Media work solely for the people of the Korrupt-Klandestine-Konspiracy! Every time a Black man or Black male teen is accused of a crime and arrested, the news media is there exclusively for one reason, which is to give him a public lynching, with their one-sided reporting of the story! Consequently, they never give the accused person an opportunity to tell his side of the story, when it is common knowledge that there are two sides to every story!

    The news media's atrocious actions are the product of a deep-seated and racially motivated Konspiracy. Moreover, their ill-actions make it much easier and simple for the jury to return a verdict of guilty. You see, most, if not all, of the time members of the jury have seen it on television news, or read about the case in the newspaper, therefore an already prejudice, bias, and malignant-hearted jury, hating the accused solely due to his Black skin, immediately develop a pre-conceived and arbitrary notion that the

Black skin makes him guilty! On that note, conviction is only a few minutes away.

Please note, that the evil and wicked ways of the news media are not new! During the days of Chattel Slavery it was called inflaming the minds of the murderous lynch mobs. Consequently, today it is called inflaming the minds of the new-lynch-mobs of twelve, better known as the jury machine! The news media's one-sided story which revolves around what the police and District Attorney said happened, is the primary reason the conviction rate is so high!

The black-hearted, evil, and wicked people of the news media will always paint a picture of the Black man and Black male teen as the villain, because the pernicious and deprated people of the Korrupt-Klandestine-Konspiracy are the Ventriloquists that control the people of the news media! They are also the ones that want the Black man removed from the planet altogether!

Made in the USA
Columbia, SC
29 June 2025